Dismantling Mr Doyle

By the same author
Home from England

James Ryan

DISMANTLING
MR DOYLE

PHOENIX HOUSE
London

First published in Great Britain in 1997 by
PHOENIX HOUSE
The Orion Publishing Group
Orion House
5 Upper St Martin's Lane
London WC2H 9EA

ISBN 1 861590 21 0 (cased)
ISBN 1 861590 85 7 (trade paperback)

Typeset by Selwood Systems Ltd, Midsomer Norton
Printed by Butler & Tanner Ltd
Frome and London

Dismantling Mr Doyle

Chapter

1

EVE EXAMINED THE other women in the departure lounge, separating those she imagined had given birth from those who had not. It was difficult to tell. Disconcerting, she thought, that a woman could do something as extraordinary as have a baby and display no outward signs of the experience.

She handed her boarding pass to the stewardess, toying with the idea of just blurting it out. 'I'm pregnant. Four months. A girl. Andrea.'

Besides the people in the clinic, Star was the only one who knew her secret. And she lived in upstate New York, over two thousand miles away. Letting her secret teeter on the brink of becoming public was a game Eve played more and more. Snatching it back was like claiming it as her own for the very first time. Andrea. Andrea. Andrea.

She stacked a carrier bag in the overhead compartment, trying to appear as normal as possible. But even the most routine movement, like walking or sitting down, required conscious thought. Andrea didn't like those high stretching movements. Eve let her arms dangle by her side for a few seconds before she reached up to close the luggage compartment. Andrea was turning out to be a person with very definite likes

1

and dislikes. Grapefruit. That was something she loved. She insisted that Eve eat it non stop.

One thing that Eve could not understand was how someone who had opted for amniocentesis could then decide that they did not want to know the gender of the baby. It didn't make sense. Surely all expectant mothers wanted to build as close a relationship as possible with their developing babies. Relating to an *it* when you could relate to a *her* or a *him* seemed detached, cold – maybe even cruel.

She was disappointed when a man, about her own age, early thirties, conspicuously identified the seat beside her as his. She enjoyed her secret more, a great deal more, among women. Happily he lined up a sheaf of reports to read, enough to last the whole journey to New York, she hoped.

In the ten years since she left, Eve often considered returning to the US for a holiday. But when it came to booking flights she invariably felt she needed something more relaxing. Friends she had made during the year she spent studying in the US had repeatedly invited her back. Ironically it was Star, the one friend with whom she had not been in contact, that she was on her way to visit.

Out of the blue last Wednesday Star had rung Eve's old family home. Mr Doyle answered and once he discovered it was someone he did not know allowed himself to sound a good deal more confused than he actually was. Mrs Doyle took the receiver and, fussed by the thought of a transatlantic call, quickly gave Eve's number.

Star rang Eve straight away and, after a very brief resumé of what she had been doing for the ten years since they last spoke, announced that she was six weeks pregnant. She told Eve she was going through her address book, systematically contacting everyone in it to tell them the news. She said it was one of a series of strategies to make the baby feel part of her world right from the beginning, explaining to Eve that it reduced the possibility of miscarriage. As soon as she could, Eve told Star

2

her own news. Andrea. Within seconds plans for a get-together were underway.

Eve tried to imagine how Star might have changed but soon became preoccupied with remembering how she herself had been when they first met. She began to jot down words. *Hopeful.* Then *innocent* – which after a little thought she crossed out and replaced with *naïve*. Then *unfocused* followed by *eager.*

These glimpses she got of herself arriving in the US ten years before began to merge, gradually forming a steady unin-terrupted narrative into which she slipped effortlessly. Soon she was feeling all the apprehension she had felt in the arrivals hall on that fetid June afternoon. All those people, moving like larvae. Thousands of them, shouting, eating, kissing, begging. And the security feds, their bulging arms folded, chewing and looking straight into people's faces. One of them, strawberry-pocked and pink-lipped, caught her eye and she smiled in response. It was an explanatory smile. She smiled a second time, trying to let him know that the first smile was a mistake. He yawned, gum stretching like stalactites from his upper teeth to the outstretched tip of his tongue, staring at her beads. Eve wanted to fasten the top two buttons of her blouse. Cotton so tissue-papery fine that the girl beside her on the plane said she knew someone who got a tan through a blouse like it. In California.

She tried to remember the name of that girl. She figured it began with B. She wrote the letter down at the end of the long list of words she had made to describe herself. She couldn't remember so she settled for Bee. Bee was heading for California but planned to check out New York first. 'A day or two, maybe more.' She said it depended on the kind of scene she hit. 'Me too,' Eve added, abandoning her plan to go directly to her college in West Virginia.

The security guard continued to look at her as she walked past. His mouth open, inside all glossy and viscid, a bit like the innards that sometimes come tightly packed inside a super-market chicken.

Eve had told Bee she'd wait for her to come through from Immigration under the People Meeting People sign. Bee had been through before, she had spent the previous year bumming around on a JI visa. Couldn't get one a second time round so she'd gone home just to get a visitor's visa. She said nobody except immigration and the Social Security people cared. By the time they caught up with you you'd've moved on some-where else. 'Movin' on, that's what America is all about,' she said slowly. Like the last line of a theorem. Brings you back to the beginning. Eve liked the way Bee made America sound easy. All those people movin' on all the time.

Somewhere backstage in Eve's thoughts, fragments of one of those movin' on songs were trying to connect up; short intermittent blasts leading to a small roomful of people sitting on the floor listening to the song. It was a place she wanted off her horizon, someone's basement flat, full of diminishing possibilities. No sign of Bee.

There was a queue for the People Finder beside her. Just key in a name and it flashed on to monitors at all the other People Meeting People points. A man bowed slightly in her direction, gesturing toward the People Finder. Pretended he thought she was waiting to use it. She tried to make herself look sour, unapproachable, the kind of person that doesn't get abducted.

New smells. Suck sweets, barley sugar and the surgical whiff from the nappy bag a woman nearby zipped open. Neatly packed, everything in separate compartments. She took out a giant tub of antiseptic cream, twisted the lid and offered it to two flat-faced little boys sitting on a stack of luggage in front of her. Each dipped a finger in and scooped up the pearly ointment. She goaded them on, like a football coach, getting them all worked up about how filthy everything was.

There in the distance was Bee. At last. Wafting along in the middle of a group, all bobbing up and down around her. Rapid, jocular chat coming from the man on her right. She laughed, throwing her head back, closing her eyes. She didn't spot Eve.

'Over here. Bee. I'm here.' Eve waved, a high, semi-circular wave.

Bee glanced over. Big smile, conspiratorial.

'Look what I ran into in baggage collection. Haven't set eyes on him since I was thirteen. Irish college. Recognised me straight away.'

Irish college, Eve thought, and the thought sank like an anchor, immobilising her in a mire of colourless memories. Wet days, speaking broken Irish, a clammy school hall, boys with big ears and breaking voices showing off to each other.

The boy-man beamed. 'Small world.'

'I thought you were in some kind of trouble with Immigration,' Eve said, and then as offhand as she could in his direction, 'Yeah. Small world.'

'We're going to Atlanta.' They looked at each other like honeymooners.

'Atlanta, Georgia,' he explained as Eve grappled with Bee's sudden change of plan.

'Yeah. I know. Georgia. Rainy Night. On My Mind.' It was a stupid reply, Eve thought, her fist clenching.

Bee drew the shoulder straps of her rucksack forward, wriggling as she pulled the collar of her jacket out.

'See ya,' she smiled. 'I have the address of that place you're going to. West Virginia, isn't it? I'll send you a card from Atlanta. By the way, this is Ciaran.'

Handshake on the way. Converted to a wave as they backed away.

Pathetic, Eve thought, being so upset saying goodbye to Bee, someone she'd only known for six hours. She wished she hadn't told Bee so much about herself. She'd emptied herself out on that flight. Plans. Dreads. The lot. And Bee wrapped it all up saying she'd send her a card from Atlanta. A card to 'that

5

place' she was going to. Bee, like everyone else in sight, was movin' on.

Eve stood beside the People Finder unsure of what to do next. Soon she was thinking about her parents and how much they had boasted about her. A post graduate scholarship, that's what she had told them. It was a way of avoiding questions about why she wanted to go. Made it seem like a big opportunity, something she couldn't turn down. And it had worked. Mr and Mrs Doyle had said the words 'a full scholarship' so often that Eve sometimes forgot the facts herself; a partial remission of fees on condition that she undertook week-end library work – those were the facts. The rest of the money came from a bank loan. A secret, so secret, that she was even inclined to keep it from herself. But now, thousands of miles away, all that secrecy seemed out of place. Suddenly she wanted to ring them and tell them the truth.

Eve keyed Bee's name into the People Finder. She knew she was on her way to Atlanta with Babyface. Everybody looking at those monitors in that airport was going to hold her name in their minds for a split second, then forget about her for ever. Eve too.

Just when she was beginning to feel good about things, she heard a familiar accent. Quick glance to the left. It was the loud mouths. She recognised them from the flight. Kept calling the hostess 'Miss', ordering cans of beer every five minutes. Made a chain with the can tabs and tried to get a girl across the aisle to put it on like a necklace. Dropped her magazine as she moved to a different seat, blushing to a chorus of 'yahoos'.

As they approached Eve they started jostling, pushing each other about. 'Take your hands off me. Queer.' Then a roar. 'Who let off?' Raucous denials.

She thought about the groups, just like them, all over the college campus at home, huddled together like cattle around troughs. Those doubts she had about what she was doing two thousands miles from home began to disappear.

6

Outside the terminal building panic stricken people tried to claw their way on to the buses before the arrivals got off. Curried food body smells, pools of congealed motor oil, people whizzing about like flies. The first stationary person Eve saw was a guy with a lemon and orange cone-shaped hat. A turquoise tassel dangled from the peak down over his eyes. He had a rat in a cage, tail whipping out through the padded rungs. Nose and whiskers, nibbling mechanically.

'Touch a rat. Stroke Roberta's Tail. 50 cents.' Shaky handwriting on jagged cardboard.

She walked by so fast that she almost tripped over a family huddled around a cake. A cluster of candles burned between the 'happy' and the 'birthday'. They were a tight little group – squeezed in together by the bustle and mill of the crowds. Nobody else looked down at them. A little boy, five maybe six, big tartan bow-tie, eyes agog. Girl a few years older in a fluffy party dress, yellow taffeta. All their clothes looked like they might have been in storage for a while. The parents smiled at each other, maybe a bit nervous but generally pleased with the arrangement. Was it their idea, Eve thought, or did the little boy actually want to have his birthday party outside an airport terminal? It struck her that they might have been on a long journey and this was the only chance they had.

Quick eye-catching glance in Eve's direction.

Most of her said move on. Definitely move on and don't stare. But at the same time she felt she'd like to stop being so cautious all the time. Bee had said she felt the same way. They had talked a lot about that on the flight – how they wanted to take risks. Not the clichéd sex risks which, they agreed, had turned out not to be risks at all. Real risks. Life risks. Bee said that in the search for Relevance you get nowhere if you don't sometimes act totally on impulse. They had both nodded.

It suddenly struck Eve – as she brushed by them – they could be refugees. Political exiles, expelled by some fascist junta for taking a stance in a civil liberties campaign somewhere. And they ended up having to have their son's birthday party on a busy thoroughfare, displaced and confused.

They bunched together, making room, all smiling with the same hopeful expression.

'You're welcome,' the father said as she dallied in front of them.

She was surprised by how well he spoke English. But figured that 'you're welcome' is one of those phrases people pick up on, day one. They hear it everywhere.

She knelt down. Just for a sec, thinking one friendly face may make a big difference here. She positioned her rucksack to act as a buffer between her and the incessant trample. Big confident beam from Birthday Boy. Big confident beam from Mom. Sister wasn't so sure.

'You're welcome at our table. You've been guided here to celebrate Eliah's birthday with us. Born right here in this very spot six years ago. We were on our way. All been ordered to register. Big census. The whole Empire. The others will be here soon.'

Eve looked around. Hoards of people. None of them stopping.

'Bearing gifts, gold, myrrh.' He sucked air through his nostrils until they caved in. 'Frankincense,' he exhaled, eyes glazing. 'Smell it.' They all leaned towards her, sniffing. Then, one by one they tanked up on the rose water she had rubbed into her hair. Heads quivered as they drew to the last.

Eve told herself she should have known what was going on as soon as he said she'd been guided. And the name. Eliah.

'Got to go. Bus to Buffalo.'

The little boy began to whimper. 'It's my birthday.'

'You can't go. Look.' The father pointed at the little boy who was whinging. Definitely a fake whinge.

'Sorry. I'm sorry but I have to go. Happy birthday.'

The father slipped his hand into a bag by his side. 'Before this day is through, before this day of days is through, you will find yourself wanting to know more.' He handed her a leaflet. One glance at the big print and she got the whole picture.

THE SECOND COMING.

Big cliché, she thought, backpacker edging away from religious weirdos promising to read a glossy handout about salvation. All the worse when she recalled how angry she used to get watching religious trappers trying to snare people on The Mall at home.

She wasn't going to Buffalo, just saw the name on a stationary bus in the distance. She had to get away from Eliah's birthday. Fast. But the lie had taken root – like when she used to try to get off school by faking illness. She remembered how she'd then start to feel ill and couldn't snap out of it even when she was on her own. Eve wondered if she would always feel she had to turn lies she told into the truth.

She continued to head towards the Buffalo bus but only because it was pulling out and she was going to miss it. Small display of disappointment. Theatre of the Absurd, Eve thought: me missing a bus I didn't intend taking.

She thought of her parents again, startled by how vivid they appeared. She wanted to ring them, tell them she'd arrived safely, hear their voices. But she was afraid she might say something stupid, like how glad she was they weren't religious weirdos. And that would have been enough to start them off. They were always on about how a drink could get spiked at a party, convinced that every time she looked away there was someone waiting to pour something into her glass that would make her take off her clothes. Even that wasn't the worst part. The worst part was the baby that would ruin your life. There was a different story altogether for her brothers.

She had to struggle to get her parents into perspective, hoping that when she did she would no longer want to ring them. It wasn't easy.

She decided to go back into the terminal building, sit down, have a coffee and take stock.

On her way across to the coffee shop she bought three postcards. When she had finished writing she went through the New York addresses she had been given, people she'd never met but whose sister or brother or friend told her to be sure and contact them if she was passing through. She figured she might have rung except what was she supposed to say when they picked up the phone? She tried to imagine what a conversation with one of them would be like. Geraldine Cassidy's cousin Adel for instance.

'Hi, Adel. I'm just passing through. I'm a friend of Ger's.' Pause. 'Ger. Geraldine Cassidy.'

'Oh yeah? How is she? Didn't get to see her when I was home in July.'

'She's doing fine.'

Eve might have gone on to say that things between her and Barry were a bit dodgy just then. But it seemed so idiotic. Ringing someone she had never met from a public phone at the airport to tell them that things between people two thousand miles away were a bit dodgy.

It was a negative mind-set and Eve was working her way out of it but in such a way as to avoid admitting she was in it.

Revert to the original plan. West Virginia.

All through the summer whenever she though about being in the States and she though about it a lot – it was different. It wasn't an airport arrivals hall with her writing postcards or her tangling with religious weirdos. It was nearly always a dark bar, thin strains of Billie Holliday wafting through the smoke, bearing witness to the worthlessness of everything – except love. Lots of slinky people soaking up her hard-earned wisdom. And the plaintive a.m. wail of a saxophone, playing to bowed heads. But there didn't seem to be a starting point. Somehow it wasn't enough just to be there. The thought occurred – and not for the first time – maybe it was her.

On the bus, late that night, Eve drifted in and out of sleep. It was a six-hour journey, spent with the side of her head bumping intermittently against the window, haphazardly thinking of changes she'd like to make to herself. Every time she got close to fixing on a definite course of action she found herself sliding back, half heartedly grasping at incidental questions. Questions she wasn't all that interested in answering – like why did she put exclamation marks after everything she wrote on those postcards?

In an inaudible whisper she said the name of the college she hoped to arrive at sometime the following morning. Raleigh Reilly. Repeating it like a mantra. Raleigh Reilly. Raleigh Reilly. Slowly the words began to regulate everything – all those stray thoughts, the hum of the engine, the pinched discomfort of the seat, jet lag and what she felt was a below average performance in New York.

Chapter

2

EVERYONE AGREED, IN a single surge of different sounds, that it was an exceptionally generous retirement present. A clear indication of Mr Doyle's popularity at Good, Good and Stavely. One thousand pounds credit at Heaslip and Molloy, Timber and Hardware Merchants, Casement Street, Cork, all spelled out in large block optician's chart capitals on an outsize gift voucher – waist high like one of those charity cheques.

'What are you going to get with it?' Inez asked, full of head-girl pep, sure she could be heard above the din of the applause.

'Thanks be to God it isn't a gold watch,' Mr Doyle nodded as he spoke, pacing the words with the nods, still beaming with pleasure at the praise his fellow directors had showered on him, and in particular the extraordinary tribute – the truly, extraordinary tribute – paid by his old sparring partner, Hugh Thornley.

His daughter-in-law decided that her question had got lost in the clatter of cups and saucers landing on the table. She spoke louder.

'Well. Tell us what are you going to get with it?' She was impatient now, running her fingers up and down the stem of her glass.

Anton watched, hoping that his father would hear his wife's

question this time. He knew she would keep on asking, getting more and more insistent until Mr Doyle answered. Anton was not always able to contain his edginess when his wife and his father spoke. She looked so expectant, always so forward with Mr Doyle, more so than anyone else in the family, agreeing and disagreeing as though they were on the same footing in the conversation.

'Everyone knows what he's going to buy with it,' Anton said, foiling Inez who had her chin raised, ready to direct the question forcibly at Mr Doyle. She glanced over at her husband, her breath still drawn, not sure if he had finished speaking, but then suddenly abandoned her question when she saw how intently he was staring at her wine glass.

'So they do now, do they? Everyone knows what I'm going to buy with it?' Mr Doyle spoke slowly, like a detective mulling over an unsatisfactory solution. He looked at them, searching their faces before lifting up the gift voucher and examining it as if it were a painting. His whole head was flushed in the heat of the low ceilinged, over-crowded room and his shirt collar was uncomfortably tight.

'See there, don't be so sure of yourself,' Inez said to Anton, imitating the tones of a school child but avoiding eye contact with him.

Anton waited stern-faced, willing her to look in his direction, which she had no intention of doing.

'Well, you haven't told me what I'm going to buy with the voucher yet.'

Mr Doyle spoke directly to Anton, one eye cocked, embedded in the furry bristle of his arched eyebrow, his most challenging expression.

Anton was, for the moment, beyond challenge, beyond seeing that his attempts to control the way his wife spoke to his father were misguided. Mr Doyle liked Inez. He enjoyed her openness, her interest in what he had to say, all that laughter. If he had been the sort of person who reflected on things he would have been quick to acknowledge how flattered he was by the unselfconscious way she flirted with him. Anton did not realise the rules were changing and that his father was more than willing to exchange the awesome respect men of his generation commanded for the sort of lively chat Inez provided.

Anton leaned back on his chair distancing himself momentarily from the imponderable ravel of chat which zigzagged in directions only the Doyles themselves could follow.

'I'd be very surprised,' he then announced so formally that everyone stopped talking, 'I'd be very surprised if this voucher didn't go towards the purchase of a drive lawnmower with all the extras.'

Mr Doyle put one hand on the table, palm facing upwards as if he were revealing a losing hand in a poker game. 'Full marks, Anton, am I that transparent?'

With his open hand pointing towards Anton, Mr Doyle generously diverted attention from himself to his main supporting actor.

'I'm only stating the obvious,' Anton smirked.

'You stating the obvious?' Syl paused. 'You stating the obvious. That's an achievement.' He leaned forward in anticipation of a return quip, which would almost certainly have followed if all eyes hadn't suddenly turned on Mrs Doyle. She was emptying the salt-cellar on a wine spill with one hand, while waving with the other, trying to attract the attention of the plump waitress over by the big vase of fleshy white lilies. As the waitress padded over, Mrs Doyle began to explain that what she was doing would save the table-cloth from becoming permanently stained. 'But it will' – and this she offered as a personal challenge to the waitress – 'need to be soaked in lukewarm water overnight.'

Everyone looked at the little mound of salt absorbing the reddish grey wine.

Eve was embarrassed. She wondered what it was about her

mother that made her do things like that. For a split second she considered pointing out that a wine spill in a big hotel is not the concern of a customer. But she knew how easily her mother could be silenced. And anyway it was too late.

Eve asked the waitress to bring two bottles of sparkling water. 'And fresh glasses,' she added, winning the waitress's attention from Mrs Doyle, who had begun to explain a way of revitalising fatigued linen. But to Eve's relief her mother seemed content enough to pass this tip on to her daughters-in-law, allowing the waitress to leave under the impression, Eve hoped, that she had been called over to get water and glasses.

'Of course, I won't be buying it until the end of season sale,' Mr Doyle announced.

All the Doyles laughed, enthusiastically lining up for one of their set pieces, with Mr Doyle's thrift as the theme and their stock responses – exasperation, outrage, incredulity – all shooting up and down the scales like a Gilbert and Sullivan chorus. He sat with his head bowed, pretending defeat, then rallied with a retort that set the whole sequence in motion again.

'You hardly think I'm going to buy a drive lawnmower in March when it'll cost twenty per cent less in October.'

While they all dived for their firing positions again, gasping and laughing, Mr Doyle quietly surveyed the room, anxious to hide how much he hoped his youngest son, Noel, had not left. During the speeches he had tried to spot him, peering over the rims of his reading glasses with his chin drawn in, almost touching his tie knot. They had met on the way in and Noel, a committed social worker, with his usual unfaltering sincerity had introduced his small ill-at-ease *new family* – three defeated, ageless men in poorly fitting overcoats – to his original family. Mr Doyle began to worry and was just about to give up when he spotted a single glass, shyly raised, in the far distance. Mr Doyle smiled his most heart-felt smile of the evening.

True to his word he waited until the October sales to buy the drive lawnmower. By that stage he had a bulging file full of glossy brochures and there was little he didn't know about the different makes. But as a matter of principle he kept an open mind, preferring to make the decision in Heaslip and Molloy on the day, accompanied by Anton and Syl.

Several times during that summer he wondered if he should be getting a drive lawnmower at all. There was nothing wrong with the lawnmower he had. Old, yes, but in fairly good working order. And keeping it that way was a challenge he enjoyed. So his satisfaction in buying a new one was clouded by the regret he felt in foregoing that challenge.

This hardship began every April when he wheeled out the mower for the first cut. He walked around it a few times carrying out his inspection with as much detachment as he could muster. Then, with his apprehension well disguised he pulled the starter cord violently. If the motor didn't engage at the first attempt, he swore at it; snarlish blasts and damns, hissed through his teeth. If it did he carefully played down his satisfaction and just nodded at it.

He always took the same cutting route, moving in ever increasing circles around the laurel clump until the rolling slope to the side of the house was finished. He then took a break, easing himself down on to the stump of a lime tree.

Sitting there on that late September afternoon he began to plot the cutting route he would take when he got his new mower. But he quickly lost interest and began to drift away, carried along by thoughts that mapped out their own course. It was so calm that even faraway sounds – gull calls and an outboard hum – filled the whole bay, resounding as though it were a vast amphitheatre. And high up there in the gods, surveying it all was Mr Doyle, beginning to sense that it was time to continue cutting, prompted by the first stirrings of hollow, alien thoughts like it's only a lawnmower.

Mr Doyle was not used to following the course of meandering thoughts. He preferred the well charted terrain of problem solving, decision making, strategy creation. The greater part of his working life had been spent perfecting those skills and there was no question about how successful he had been. Reflection, or for that matter, any loose unstructured thinking was, he considered, a bad habit of mind, the enemy of decisive action. But with retirement came long days with no pressing decisions to make, days when, despite his determination, he drifted helplessly into the slipstreams of unfocused thought.

He took his hat off and ran the palm of his hand from his forehead to the nape of his neck. He held the hat at arm's length, examining it as if it belonged to someone else. He then began to brush the mowed flecks off the cream linen, chuckling a little to himself as he recalled how, goaded on by Mrs Doyle, he had bought the hat the previous April in Istanbul. Designed for wear in the tropics, it had muslin vents on both sides which the stall owner in the bazaar said, and repeated dozens of times with the same fixed smile, were to 'permit the entry of the air'.

It had been the cruise of a lifetime, no doubt about that. He almost said it out loud and then without thinking turned to look for Mrs Doyle, who as often as not was looking out of the big kitchen window while she pottered at the sink. She was there and quick to laugh when he pointed mockingly to the vents in his hat.

'To permit the entry of the air,' he mouthed in the distance, exaggerating the shape of each word until his facial movements came to resemble those of an opera singer.

She dismissed it all with a head shake and a smile so pert that to someone who did not know her she might well have appeared cross.

Nothing was ever a problem to Syl Doyle's secretary, Miranda. She was unshakeably confident, *au fait* with all the latest technology, breezy and expert at resisting the senior secretaries' unending attempts to point out the pecking order in the office. She called him by his first name, sometimes playfully extending it to Sylvester. And to the audible discomfort of the senior secretaries – a scratchy sound as they recrossed their legs – she often replied to his passing 'Hi-how's-things' with a thinly veiled reference to her menstrual cycle.

When he flew out of his office that morning he didn't stop or even look in Miranda's direction.

'I'll be in Heaslip and Molloy's. Have me paged in half an hour. Make it sound urgent.'

Anton, every bit as busy as Syl, and to his own way of thinking busier, arrived at Heaslip and Molloy ahead of time but not before his father. That sort of carry on, good-humoured one-upmanship, didn't bother him as much as it might have done a year or two previously. It wasn't as if they had moved beyond all that brinkmanship, it was just that the occasional chink had begun to appear in Mr Doyle's armour, putting Anton at an uncomfortable advantage. But decades of picking his steps carefully around Mr Doyle left him unable to assume that ease which made all his brother Syl's dealings with him seem direct and unguarded.

With Syl it had been less complex all along. Mr Doyle just pointed at the finishing tape and then fired the starting gun. And while he occasionally hollered instructions he was so preoccupied with Anton's progress that Syl was free to make his way forward at his own pace. This he did at a gallop expecting for a long time that with each new success – exams, big job, promotion – he might join Anton centre stage. It never happened nor could it ever happen. It was as if the Doyles believed that in Anton they had provided the others with a blueprint for success. In that way, he was credited, in part, for all achievements chalked up by the rest of the family.

This became most apparent when, with friends, the talk came around to how their various children were faring. When it was well underway the Doyles might often be found teasing one another, each jocosely asserting that Anton's brilliance came from their side, while the family shortcomings, which they could never quite pinpoint, came from the other. It was a routine their friends could easily have found tiresome. But more often than not those friends lost track of what was being said, distracted by the way Mr Doyle let go of all self-possession, overcome by a child-like, uninhibited pride whenever he spoke of Anton's achievement. About the only person who never heard him speak in this way was Anton. This was not out of any kind of begrudgery, but because Mr Doyle believed that the way Mrs Doyle constantly fussed over Anton more than adequately displayed their collective satisfaction in him.

Mr Doyle stood in a clearing in the middle of Heaslip and Molloy, his chin raised and his head moving as though he was looking for someone in particular. He enjoyed outings that had any kind of tribal feel to them, which was why Anton and Syl had agreed to go. They stood a few paces away and observed their father with the same boyish awkwardness, knowing all along they would have little or no part to play in the transaction. But keen to stand their own ground they launched into conversation, pointing out to each other how frustrating they had found leaving their offices just when they were beginning to make some headway. Still, as they chatted each found a way to let the other know that despite all the difficulties they were at no point tempted to let their father down.

A lanky young sales assistant approached. 'Can I ...' then, mid-sentence seemed to lose confidence, giving way to Mr Doyle.

'I'd like to see the sales director. Doyle is the name.'

The assistant wavered for a moment before backing away from Mr Doyle's very firm smile.

Mr Doyle did not need to turn around to explain to Anton and Syl that he wasn't going to do business with a young counter jumper. They knew too well what was going on and were already raising their eyes in anticipation of what was to come. Then, slightly surprising each other, they smiled, finding themselves, once again with their father, hopelessly stranded between exasperation and affection.

Mr Doyle's demand to see the sales director had triggered off a whole series of 'call-the-manager' memories which, to Anton's surprise, no longer made him squirm.

Grinning a little to himself, Anton approached Syl who had drifted over to the home decoration section. Within seconds they were laughing so much that Mr Doyle, waiting at some distance for the arrival of the sales director, turned around to see what was going on.

'I'd forgotten completely about that,' Syl was saying, taking off his glasses and rubbing his eyes as Anton described the atmosphere in the hotel dining-room in Brittany almost fifteen years before. It was a call-the-manager episode surpassing all others.

A large platter of fruit was placed in the centre of their table after dinner. In a series of very slick movements the waiter made a few on-the-spot adjustments to the arrangement, moving the bananas slightly closer to the nectarines, tilting the angle at which a pear stood, then with a magician-like flourish and a quick twitch of a smile he disappeared. The Doyles stared at the fruit. It had a still-life quality, arranged as if it were about to be painted.

'Look. A real pineapple. I wonder if it tastes different. I mean different to tinned pineapple.' Mrs Doyle leaned forward to look more closely at what was unmistakably the *pièce de résistance* of the display.

'What's that piece of paper? What's written on it?' Mr Doyle pointed at a small card fixed with a cocktail stick to the frosted aquamarine leaves at the top of the pineapple.

'*Ne coupez pas, s'il vous plait,*' Eve read, leaving big intervals between each word.

'What? What's it saying?'

'Do not cut,' Anton replied.

'Do not cut? Show it to me,' Mr Doyle barked, his hand stretching out to take the card.

One quick glance at it and his chin shot up, his face tensing with impatience as he beckoned the waiter.

'Waiter, we need a large knife please,' Mr Doyle held the pineapple up with one hand and pointed at it with the other. 'A knife,' he repeated, as the waiter approached from the nearby service area.

The waiter, thinking that they did not understand the *Ne coupez pas* instruction, harnessed his entire body to say '*Non*'. His head shook, the index fingers of both his upheld hands wagged mechanically and his eyes bulged out of their sockets. So when he said, '*Il ne faut pas le toucher*,' it seemed to the Doyles that he was repeating himself.

'Deesplay,' he added, searching Mrs Doyle's face for reassurance.

'You see, we come from a country,' she began, 'where pineapples don't...'

'It's got nothing to do with that,' Mr Doyle scowled at her. 'Now could we have a knife please'.

The waiter stood there unsure of what to do.

'I'd like to speak to the manager.'

From then on it was plain sailing. The manager arrived, smiling, whisked the pineapple out of Mr Doyle's hand and, watched by the Doyles, the other guests in the dining-room as well as the sniggering kitchen staff who crowded the service hatch, dramatically cut it into six large slices. He then clicked his fingers at the waiter who was already on the way with dessert plates.

'I haven't eaten pineapple since,' Syl bunched his lips, grimacing with exaggerated revulsion.

The sales director arrived and shook hands with Mr Doyle, but they had barely begun speaking when the lanky assistant strode up to them and after a quick exchange led Mr Doyle away.

'He must be losing his touch,' Syl spoke without moving his mouth, as he and Anton headed over to the small office into which the sales assistant had ushered Mr Doyle.

The door was slightly open but even if it hadn't been Mr Doyle's voice would have sounded every bit as clear because of his habit of shouting into telephones.

'How urgent?' they heard him demand. 'Well it'll have to be cancelled – you'll have to find a way of cancelling it. He's on family business and he won't be back until after lunch. That could be three o'clock.'

He handed the receiver to the lanky assistant who was so taken by the authority with which Mr Doyle went about things that he waited for the go-ahead before putting it back in its place.

'Thank you,' Mr Doyle said, smiling magnanimously. The assistant stood back, shoulders pressed against the wall, holding himself in to let Mr Doyle pass.

Outside Syl and Anton were waiting, both rapidly running out of whatever it was that, until then, had made it possible to laugh.

'Well, you've just had a narrow escape. Skin of your teeth. They wanted you to go back at the office.'

Sly looked at his father sheepishly, knowing there was more to come.

'That Miss of a secretary of yours nearly didn't take no for an answer.'

'Miranda.' Syl semi stammered, wondering why he was telling his father his secretary's name. But he quickly bounced back and before long was scrutinising his father as objectively as a son could, asking himself if the man was a knowing participant in the battle of wits in which he seemed to be permanently engaged.

'Miranda,' Mr Doyle said, making his way over to the sales director and repeating the name as if it explained her behaviour. Syl and Anton trooped behind but had to quicken their step as Mr Doyle and the sales director headed for the heavy rubber swing doors leading to the warehouses.

After a long walk through a maze of dimly lit, creosote smelling store rooms which included traipsing up a steep metal staircase and then down a series of concrete steps, they arrived in a well lit showroom full of gardening equipment. Electric hedge cutters, rotavators, fertiliser dispensers, chainsaws and dozens of lawnmowers all arranged to fan out from a gleaming red drive mower.

Anton and Syl were not in the least surprised when he began – breathless after the trek – by asking about ordinary power mowers. He wanted to let the sales director introduce the idea of a drive mower and then reluctantly allow himself to be talked into buying it. It was one of his many bargaining tactics. Having Anton and Syl there was another. He went back and forth to them several times, giving the sales director the impression that he had to get the go-ahead from them. Swept along by his excitement, they gave little thought to their own, much discussed, criticisms of his way of doing business. They had often joked about how out-of-line it was with con-temporary practice. It wasn't about money, it was about out-manoeuvring the opponent, whom Mr Doyle believed beyond a shadow of a doubt was always intent on outmanoeuvring him.

The sales director stood by patiently while Mr Doyle tried the drive lawnmower seat for comfort, wriggling much more than was necessary. He gripped the steering wheel with both hands and with his brow furrowed concentrated on the dis-tance ahead, pretending to drive. After he had successfully swung the machine around an imaginary corner he waved over to Syl and Anton. It was the sort of thing he did a lot when they were younger, believing that he was teaching them not to be daunted by the world. Anton looked on, knowing that his indulgent smile was a cruel refusal to play but nonetheless determined to hold on to it. Syl checked his watch compulsively.

Finally after a marathon session which, as it neared its closing stages, took on the physical intimacy of a loose ruck, the lawnmower was bought. The sales director, exhausted by Mr Doyle's antics, still managed to joke and laugh all the way back to the front section of the shop.

'We did well. He didn't know what he was up against when he saw us first.' Mr Doyle's voice was full of triumph as they crossed Casement Street on their way to lunch.

Us? Anton thought. Who's 'Us'? He thought of Inez and their daughter Sabina and wondered if he would always be included in his father's 'us'.

Questions about where he himself stood in the scheme of things never bothered Mr Doyle. To him it was, and always would be, 'us' – the Doyles in combat with the world. And with himself at the helm, Mr Doyle felt they were doing better than most.

Chapter

3

OF THE THOUSANDS, hundreds of thousands of Irish Americans who at the turn of the century had their sights set on college educations for their sons, none could have been more determined than Tom Reilly, Chairman of Thomas P. Reilly and Son. Earthworks Inc. A degree from an Ivy League college for his only son, that's what he wanted for Thomas P. Jr. – and wanted with the same hell-bent determination which had got him everything else.

His company had major projects underway in seven states, locally supervised, for the most part, by young eager bow-tied college-educated engineers. 'Not bad, not bad at all for a man who only knows the letters of his own name,' he would boast to his young son. He so frequently imagined the boy in a cap and gown, scroll in hand, that he failed to see that there might be reasons why even the least discerning of the Ivy League colleges would turn his son down.

When, many years later, this did happen Thomas P. Reilly set about suing the colleges, ending up in the Supreme Court. Every stage of the case was widely publicised, prompting dozens of letters of encouragement to Thomas P. Reilly.

Days before the final hearing, a very formal letter arrived

from a Professor Jobe Smith who proposed that Thomas P. Reilly should build his own university and humbly offered his services in setting it up. Reilly, encouraged by his lawyers, was convinced he was going to win his case and gave Professor Jobe Smith's proposal scant consideration. But the idea took hold and in the unrelenting gloom of his Supreme Court failure, it began to surface.

Jobe Smith was summoned and within a short time of his arrival at Reilly's home was informally appointed president of Thomas P. Reilly College. It would be, they told each other passionately, a university better than the best the Union had to offer.

The foundation stone was laid in December 1926. A photograph of the bronze plaque commemorating the event decorated the back cover of the college prospectus which came with Eve's acceptance letter.

The name Raleigh was introduced by Professor Smith to emphasise what he presented to Reilly as the 'historical dimension' of the college. The site, on the lower slopes of the Blue Ridge Mountains, was part of that vast tract of land which had been granted by Elizabeth I to Sir Walter Raleigh. Significantly, the windowless bothán in East Cork from which the Reillys had been evicted when Thomas P. was eight, also stood on a tract of land – though by no means as extensive – which, three hundred years previously, had been granted by Elizabeth to Raleigh. Reilly was uneasy about the connection but much as he scratched his head he couldn't say why. Professor Smith won the day.

In 1928, Reilly was one of the few construction industry tycoons to figure that the slump in business that winter was different to the usual seasonal dip. With Reilly it was more a hunch than anything else. And because he always acted on hunches he began to tread cautiously. When, by the summer of the following year, business had not picked up he set about taking definite steps to protect his company. The first was to scale down considerably the college construction programme. But he agreed to let Professor Smith begin teaching in the north wing of the Humanities building, the only portion anywhere near completion.

Professor Smith's specialisation was dreams. He had started recording and cataloguing dreams at the turn of the century and had thousands of them, meticulously documented in his minuscule handwriting. The main thrust of his work centred on the belief that the same or similar characters stalk the dreams of all humans, usually disguised in the personae of people the dreamer knows. He had an ardent following in a St Louis suburb where, until he was appointed president of Raleigh Reilly College, he had ministered to a closely knit splinter group of the Episcopalian Church. Initially it was called The Church of Nocturnal Truth but the name was subsequently changed to The Church of Jobe Smith. Four leading members of that congregation, three women and a man, all in late middle age, became the first students to enrol at Raleigh Reilly. They arrived in September 1929 for a week-long course promising 'to promote fluency in the language of dreams'. They were advised to bring their own reclining chairs to the lecture theatre 'to safeguard', the prospectus warned, 'against the occurrence of bodily injury, should a student faint as frequently happens during Professor Smith's very moving talks on the language of dreams'.

The crash that October brought the Raleigh Reilly building programme to a complete standstill. But under Jobe Smith's direction the college struggled on through the depression years as the American Foundation for the Cataloguing and Recording of Dreams. During the summer months it was rented to a consortium of societies investigating paranormal phenomena. They set a high value on the glaring incompleteness of the building which, with its five great Doric columns supporting a portal and nothing else, looked like a movie set for a Biblical epic. For over half a century these massive columns and the low Humanities wing to the left were all there was of Raleigh Reilly.

The discovery in 1980 of the Jobe Smith *Dream Journals* by Martha Seers, a Neo-Jungian scholar and practising psychotherapist, marked the beginning of a new phase in the history of the college. The 'find', 11,200 meticulously recorded dreams, was compared in *Psychosearch* to the discovery of the Tutankhamun tomb. Their particular value was the insight they provided into the subconscious world of pre-suffragette women. Raleigh Reilly was suddenly on the academic map.

An assortment of developers, realising the commercial potential of the college, bought the entire four-hundred-acre campus site from Thomas P. Reilly's heir, Thomas Jr. who administered his dwindling estate from his poolside in New Jersey.

Soon the five great columns had become the imposing front of a new Behavioural Sciences block. To mark this new beginning, three one-off scholarships were offered to persons native to those places with which the college had historical links. St Louis, birthplace of Jobe Smith, East Walpole, Mass., home of Thomas P. Reilly and the townsland in which he was born, Cashelcurren Co. Cork. The Irish scholarship was awarded to Sadie Fields who spent two years in Raleigh Reilly before returning to Ireland to take up a university lectureship. Among those students who signed up for her first tutorial group that autumn was Eve.

Sadie Fields spoke of Raleigh Reilly non stop. Her enthusiasm for the place was infectious, but what led Eve to fix her sights on going there was not so much Sadie Field's enthusiasm as Sadie Fields herself. Eve wanted to be Sadie Fields. She wanted her self possession, her opinions, her surety – the distance she kept from ordinariness. She wanted to glide around the campus in clothes that made her look willowy. She wanted to stand, as Sadie Fields stood, firmly in a world of her own making.

*

The extensive building programme undertaken by the new owners of Raleigh Reilly was almost complete when Eve arrived. The only department in temporary accommodation was Equality Studies. It was located in a series of wooden buildings behind the sports centre. They could easily have been mistaken for construction huts, particularly as the nearby bleached site of the new sports emporium was still strewn with construction debris.

Inside it was like any other department, official – despite the large glossy poster of a baby seal and the papier mâché sunflower.

'You were trying to get in contact with me.' Eve stood in front of the secretary's desk, casting the words like a fly fisher, 'The secretary in the sociology department said you were trying to contact me.'

A head of springy beach-blonde hair swayed up from the big black box of a typewriter. There was an adjustment interval before the woman began to grope the air as though she were playing blindman's buff.

'Better not say who you are 'til I'm ready to write your name . . .'

There was more to follow, but she'd started to hum between the words, '. . . hmmmmm . . . ballpoint . . . hmmmm . . . memo block . . . hmmmm . . . almost there.' With the back of her hand she gently pushed an empty yoghurt carton aside to make room for her spiral pad. Every move was planned in advance.

'Go on. You can say your name now.'

Eve repeated her name but decided to hold back on the Eve abbreviation.

The hissing sound was on its way to becoming 'spell Yvonne' when Eve intervened, 'Y-V-O-N-N-E'.

The secretary wrote it down, looking at it from different angles and then, half smiling, pleased with the result said, 'You know that's about the prettiest name I've ever heard.'

'It's French.' Eve was on familiar ground, talking about her name, recalling the way her French teacher extended and curled the 'onne' bit and at the same time wondering if it was too late to say thank you.

'You French?'

'No, Irish.' She smiled in anticipation.

'My mother is going to love that. She really likes Irish people, she works mornings here and I work afternoons. Except when we swap.' She pointed at the sunflower, a gesture that Eve tried to relate to the swapping arrangement until she realised that a lot of the secretary's gestures were unrelated to what she was saying.

'It means that during the day we only get to see each other at lunch time, baton change we call it.' She arched her mouth and nodded, resigned to her lot. 'That's the way the cookie crumbles. My mother hasn't been too well. I worry a lot about her, you know. A lot.'

Eve couldn't believe how quick people were to disclose the details of their lives. It didn't matter where they were – laundromats, queues, elevators – they just started talking about themselves, their marriages, new apartments, runaway children, favourite food – whatever. They seemed strangely detached from the selves they spoke about which made Eve unsure of how she ought to respond. What, for instance, should she say to someone she'd just met who was very concerned about their mother's illness?

What kind of illness? When people are vague does it mean that the illness is terminal?

'I'm sorry.' Eve tried out an understanding nod.

'Oh no – she's not unwell, *unwell*, like seriously unwell. It's just that lately she's been dipping a little.'

Eve knew what she meant by 'dipping a little'. Out of sorts. Off form. Not herself. But no matter how many similar phrases she came up with she couldn't rid herself of an image from a film she had seen at school; a scene in which a very stressed woman rushes out of a steamy kitchen where her children are tucking into sausages and beans, tears upstairs and with her back pressed firmly against the lavatory door gluggs from an upturned bottle labelled Titanic Sherry.

'She'll be here in the morning. All morning. Like I told you she works mornings. Maybe you should call back then. I don't know why she asked you to drop by. Look here, look,' the glossy, finely manicured nail of her index finger moved slowly down a long list of names stapled to the cover of a green folder. 'You're not registered for any of our courses. Have you applied?'

'No,' Eve said. 'I didn't know there was such a department until the secretary over at Sociology told me you have been trying to contact me.'

The humming started again ... my mother didn't say anything about it ... hmmmm ... we go through everything together after dinner ... hmmmm ... the best thing is if you call by in the morning, any morning.

Eve agreed and the secretary realigned herself, moved her chair closer to her desk, collapsing rhythmically into a typing stoop.

Eve strolled back to the Behavioural Sciences building, fingers stuffed into the back pockets of her jeans, pleased that with one shoulder shrug she was able to shake off any responsibility for the confusion in the Equality Studies office. That, she told herself, was progress, very definite progress, refusing to take one whit of responsibility for the confusion created by other people.

She was less than a week at Raleigh Reilly and she knew dozens of people, all welcoming. She moved from one to the next at the beginning-of-term get-to-know-you faculty parties like someone on a shopping spree, selecting attitudes, fixing on phrases, listening to theories, mesmerised by the possibilities opening up all around her.

Then there was Star, her room-mate. The moment they met she described herself to Eve as a people person. Loved meeting them. Loved talking to them. Loved looking at them, loved almost everything about them, even what they liked to eat and drink, favourite movies, their hopes for the world. Problems. And it turned out to be true. More or less. Star spent a great deal of time flying about the campus, meeting people. Lots of them came to see her too, some in good shape, others in bits.

To Eve Star seemed to be marching through life, occupying all available space. She had targets and schedules and knew exactly what she wanted, not just at some future point but at every moment of every day.

It was almost midnight when Star tumbled in. Feet up straight away, bushed. She'd met someone called Annie Yun who'd been getting hate mail. She'd seen some of it. Wild. Poisonous stuff. They'd been working all evening on possible sources.

'But who knows? There are some really confused people out there.' Star half warned half observed, peering at the cigarette paper, trying to make out which side the thin adhesive strip was on.

'Yeah, I know. I met one of them today. Secretary in Equality Studies.'

Eve wanted to backtrack, say she was being unfair, but Star appeared so interested that Eve just forged ahead.

'Confused,' she said, stretching the word out and undulating the syllables as Star had done. 'She told me I'd have to come back some other time. She couldn't cope.' Eve's voice began to trail off. 'Something to do with her mother.'

'There are some really confused people out there,' Star drawled, sensing the lack of potential in the story, slipping the Ry Cooder album she played all the time out of its sleeve.

'Some very confused people.' Eve laughed, edging the conversation to a point where it could crumble by agreement. Then she laughed louder as Star flung her head back theatrically, faking alarm at a seed pop.

It took Eve a long time to get used to the way Star led the

direction their conversations took. If she was interested she had a way of remaining as expectant at the end of a conversation as she had been at the beginning. She gave the definite impression that she thought there ought to be more and Eve, like most people, responded by trying to provide more. They talked on, reworking what they had said in an effort to meet Star's expectations. But because there was no arrival point, no moment when Star's expression became less expectant, Eve learned to bail out. Once she had grasped the pattern she began to experiment, intrigued by the notion that by taking certain steps she could take charge of the course of a conversation. But such steps, measuring the amount of reassurance she gave, were not easy to take. She was in the habit of agreeing whole-heartedly with everything people said to her, denying them that agreement was at absolute odds with everything she had been taught.

Mid morning the day after Eve's visit to the Equality Studies dept., a hand-written letter arrived in the internal mail. It read like a personal invitation, signed Elizabeth, Equality Studies, Secretary.

Eve examined the handwriting, noting that it was totally different to the big circular script with which the secretary had written her name down.

'Her mother.' Eve mumbled as she read the letter, adding, 'Elizabeth must be her mother,' when she had finished.

Star didn't appear to have heard her. She was absorbed in the intricacies of a macramé sandal she was making for herself.

Out of the blue a minute or two later she said, 'They must really want you over there.' She looked up, wide-eyed, intro-ducing an exaggerated note of suspense as though she were reading aloud from a children's story book. Then with her hands held close to her face like claws she launched into a version of 'Goldilocks and the Three Bears', weaving what she claimed was a 'dykish plot' through the story.

Later that morning with Star's big-enough-to-eat-you voice

still ringing in her ears, Eve walked into the Equality Studies office.

'Oh good. You got my letter,' Elizabeth said. 'Thank you for dropping by.' She had a hoarse, throaty voice, full bandage-pink make-up caked very slightly at the edge of her hair line.

'You called by yesterday. You know I left details for Haley – Haley, you met Haley yesterday – I left details about students we've been trying to contact. Right here.' She pointed to a file on the desk. 'I went through it all with her at our briefing session after dinner, night before last. Your name came up. I remember reading it out. But she didn't pick up on any of it. It worries me, you know, and she's been doing so well.'

Eve looked puzzled.

'Yes, things have been difficult for Haley. We came here a year ago last April,' she paused to take a tatty envelope out of a drawer to her right, then seemed to change tack. 'I advertised in *Choice*.' Eve was listening, but not following. She took the piece of paper Elizabeth held out, with a hopeful expression as if everything would become clear once Eve had read it.

It was a column of small print advertisements with the word Choice and the date written in the margin in Elizabeth's copperplate handwriting. About half way down, circled in black, was an advertisement which read: *Secretarial Team, Mother (Elizabeth) and daughter (Haley) available as a single secretary requiring a single salary.*

Eve looked directly into Elizabeth's owlish bifocals, momentarily fascinated by the way they magnified her eyelashes, making them look like the spikes of a tropical fish. Elizabeth interpreted Eve's fascination with her eyes as interest in Haley's life story and began to sort through the contents of the envelope, picking out photographs. She handed the first of these to Eve and waited as if a particular response was called for.

It was a poor-quality gloss photograph of clothes laid out on a neatly made bed. These clothes, mainly couture suits, looked like they might have been assembled by the police – evidence connected with some sinister crime. Eve felt she was under pressure to make some sense of it and combed the photograph for clues. The suits were dated, gimmicky and slightly comical in the way fashionable clothes from another decade often are. A petrol blue suit neatly set out with the jacket lying a few inches above the skirt, a lemon suit to the right, same cut. On the other side a black cocktail dress with a curving neckline sheathed with charcoal coloured gauze.

It was time to say something but Eve was still at a loss to know what so she just said 'nice'.

Another photograph. Hats. Small pillboxes spread out like cakes on a recipe book cover.

'That's how smart Haley was. You better believe it. With that cute little hat and that classy blue number, you know, she was number one in the agency, organising conventions. You name it.'

She held her hand out for the photographs which Eve returned, feeling she had in some inexplicable way failed Haley's mother.

'I know Haley will never wear those clothes again but I'm hanging on to them anyway. It helps to remember the sort of person she once was.'

Eve was trying to think of a tactful way of asking what had happened when Elizabeth shuddered and drew the top of her pearl studded cardigan up to her chin. Suddenly she was a receptionist. Smiling, with a cheerful-against-the-odds expression.

'You wrote asking me to call by,' Eve reminded her.

'Oh yes. Yes. This time of year we go through the post-grad register.' Her smile broadened until the crimson Cupid's bow of her upper lip evened out into a straight line. 'That way we get to know what non-nationals there are on campus. You see,' Elizabeth paused, as if Eve was about to ask a question, 'you see, one of the courses we're offering, a Cross Cultural Comparative

Study of Women's Experience, is open to Inter D Masters students, with full subsid credits on offer.'

Eve, preoccupied by how charged with competence Elizabeth's voice had become, nodded, but regretting straight away that she had not conveyed her genuine interest in the course, said 'right' and then 'yeah'.

'We thought you might be interested. Nearly all non-national Inter D Masters women students are. You haven't selected your two subsids yet, have you?'

Eve shook her head.

'Assessment for this course is not based on term papers. Come the end of next semester,' Elizabeth's voice rose melodically, gauged to plateau once she hit the certainty note, 'you're going to be very busy writing those papers. Psychology, Sociology, Anthropology. My. What a handful.'

'How is the course...?'

'Assessed? Participation and some field work. But no term papers.'

Suddenly Eve was juggling her interest in what Elizabeth was saying with a memory of standing in Sister Benedicta's office, her eyes dazzled by the reflection of sunlight on a mahogany table so highly polished that its original sweet sherry colour had become a white sheen. She had gone to ask if she could drop out of the school production of 'The Sound of Music', but could not bring herself to say so. Slowly she had backed towards the door, leaving without saying anything.

Elizabeth sat chin upright, poised for a reply, while Eve, suddenly despairing of ever being able to speak with certainty on her own behalf, nodded and smiled and said yes. Then, conscious of how much she meant it, said yes again.

'Oh I am glad. That makes nine, one short of the minimum, to get the course up and running. But I'm sure that's not going to be ... you see I have a particular interest in filling this course. Haley needs to meet some people here, needs to make friends so she's going to join some of the sessions. You'd never believe,' she pointed confidentially at two doors behind Eve, 'how helpful they've been about Haley.'

Written on a perspex plaque on the door to the left was Nancy Alldice, Co-ordinator. Dept. of Equality Studies and next door, Irma Knoll, Registrar, Dept of Equality Studies.

On the way back to the Behavioural Sciences block Eve began making a list. All the positive points about being in Raleigh Reilly. It was a routine she began at least once a day, using her fingers to mark them off. People. Courses. The whole can-do atmosphere of the place. Then she would develop those positive points into full sentences, preparing yet again for the moment when she was going to sit down and write to Eugene. She knew she would have to sooner or later. He had already written a bulky four-page letter full of questions. As a display of indifference she left it in the mail box she shared with Star until the following afternoon. But that didn't work out the way she hoped. It required too much determination to feel like real indifference. Every time she passed the mail box she looked in at the letter, poking it as a child looking for signs of life might poke a dead bird. It was too subtle a gesture for Star. She only got interested in things when she could get down to brass tacks immediately.

By the time Eve opened the letter she realised that if she wanted to involve Star, which she did, she would have to be much more direct. And why not, she thought, it might just be that simple. There and then looking at the three large Xs under Eugene's name she took the decision and straight away set about putting it into practice. As soon as Star heard the words 'break up' followed by 'impossible' she dived right in.

'You want to leave him? Just go ahead. Tell him, that's it, you're through.'

'It's more complicated than that,' Eve said, apologetically, immediately wondering why.

'How much more complicated? Are you in love with him?'

Eve liked Star's shoot-from-the-hip approach but felt out-paced.

'No. At least not any more. But I don't know what to say to him about it. I don't know what happened.'

'Where did you get the idea that you have to explain to someone why you're not in love with them. For Christ's sake. Maybe nothing happened,' Star said, racing on to the next possibility, 'maybe he's just a creep.'

'Creep? No,' Eve said, trying not to lose sight of what Star had said just before; maybe nothing happened.

That's it, she almost said aloud, nothing happened and nothing was ever going to happen. They would be the same in twenty, thirty, forty, fifty years as they were then.

'Maybe he's a psychopath,' Star laughed, 'waiting to cut you up into little pieces and put you into the freezer with all his other girlfriends.'

'I'm the only girlfriend he's ever had,' Eve said, aware that such a literal reply was out of place, but at the same time keen to follow through with the facts which, since she began telling them to Star, seemed unrecognisably flat. A whole life, punctuated by Baptisms, Communions, Confirmations and endless Sunday lunches tore across her horizon, quick as flaring fuse wire.

'We've been going out since we were fifteen.'

'How long is that? Six? Seven years? It sounds to me like . . .' Star paused, incredulous, 'it sound to me like . . . I don't know.' She looked right into Eve's face, as if to imply that Eve was holding back on something, which she wasn't.

'Neither do I.' The conversation was losing momentum.

Star then launched into a story about a girl, someone called Cherry, in her high school class who ended up a complete mess because she had married her high school boyfriend, Doug or Chuck, she couldn't remember his name. Eve listened, brimming with interest, all the time concealing the mild wave of panic she felt when she remembered how at her twenty-first birthday party in the yacht club one of Eugene's friends said everyone was sure she and Eugene were going to announce their engagement later that evening. Fielding that panic, Eve lost the drift of the conversation, re-entering at the point where Star was telling her that in societies with a short life expectancy monogamy is common from the onset of fertility.

'Do Irish people have a short life expectancy?'

'No. Average to above average. I think.' Eve laughed, resigned to the impossibility of bridging the gap.

'Brad. That was his name. Brad Swaltz. The one who married Cherry Deloy. She was caught leaving a liquor store with a bottle of Bourbon stuffed into one of her kids' sou'westers. She had three kids by the time she was twenty-two and he sold the trailer they lived in before he disappeared for ever. Can you believe that?'

Even if it wasn't possible to explain all the ins and outs of the Eugene saga to Star, Eve enjoyed and, as the term went on more than enjoyed, loved talking to Star about it. She was wildly partisan, always ready to dictate what she called the 'get lost' letter. She had lots of stories like the one about Cherry Deloy and Brad Swaltz which made Eve feel less guilty about all the plotting she had done over the previous eighteen months to escape.

Chapter

4

STANDING AT THE edge of the ever-spreading laurel copse with his professional capacity long-handled pruning sheers held loosely – almost touching the ground – Mr Doyle was trying to remember who it was said that once he retired every day would be like Saturday. A bit of sailing, a spot of golf. Take your pick, weather permitting. Whoever it was, Mr Doyle thought, didn't know what they were talking about. Saturday remained Saturday, Sunday remained Sunday and the other days of the week just remained days of the week.

'No point,' he'd said dismissively, when Mrs Doyle, anxious to give the impression that she was not speaking to anyone in particular, observed that it looked like a good day for a game of golf.

'Nobody worth playing with.' He thought of the old men sitting on the wrought iron seat outside the club house and the mid-morning women golfers. 'Anyway, look at those laurels, they're beginning to block the view.'

Both looked out of the huge, clear kitchen window, gauging the extent to which the laurels had encroached on their unrivalled view of the bay.

The house had a Christmas cake look to it – a white Mediterranean-style bungalow with three hacienda arches to the right of the porch, iced all over with swirls of adobe plaster. It was called The Acre, a name first used when negotiations were going on for the site and from then adopted on by default. Mrs Doyle considered it a misleading name, creating the impression of hens foraging in a field beside a cottage. She had been on the look out for a different name from the day they moved in. For years afterwards whenever the Doyles were on a car journey together they played a game, a sort of competition, spotting potential house names and giving them marks out of ten. But The Acre went on being The Acre except for a period of about eighteen months when Mrs Doyle let Anton change it to Zanadu. Mr Doyle scoffed at the name, said people would call it the Zoo and bring monkey nuts when they came to visit. The Zoo theme was mercilessly exploited by Mr Doyle to taunt Anton about his 'primate fringe' and his 'jungle music' and so the name was gradually abandoned.

Solidarity of the sort Mrs Doyle had shown with Anton in those years often made Mr Doyle's lips curl with displeasure. He accused her of molly-coddling the boys and particularly Anton whose welfare, it seemed to him, she often considered over and above his own. He frequently complained of their lack of gratitude, privately telling Mrs Doyle that Anton was not only ungrateful but contemptuous of his efforts to provide their privileged way of life. She always consoled him in the same way, explaining Anton's defiance in the terms Mr Doyle understood best – pointing out how, despite appearances, their eldest son was very like Mr Doyle himself. In the same way she explained to Anton that his father's attempts at humiliating him were the result of a hot-headed temperament and that Mr Doyle was always more upset than Anton after one of their bouts. Like a lot of pivotal people she not only tolerated but tacitly encouraged the whimsical carry-on of the men in her care.

Mrs Doyle heaved two bulging supermarket bags on to the counter, continuing to grip the tops firmly while she paused to draw breath. Outside in the fading light Mr Doyle was still tearing and hacking his way through the laurels. She watched him charge into the copse, spreading his arms to maximise the girth the sheers could grip before forcing the handles with all his strength. He tugged and twisted like a dog pulling flesh off a bone, eventually reversing out, dragging a laurel clump the size of a small tree. Now and then he stood back to take a look, staring motionless for a moment or two, tilting his head to minimise the flaw he had spotted in the shape of the laurels. Mrs Doyle understood precisely what was going on when he stood back and she felt his frustration, as she often did, more intensely than she ever felt her own. So accurately did she track his line of thought that while he stood poised to have another go at the laurels she too stood poised in sympathy, her hand inside a chicken waiting to release a fistful of stuffing.

On and off she watched until all that remained of the laurels was a series of stumps, each one like a lone molar sticking out of an ancient gum, damp and raw in the October moonlight.

In the past she would have intervened, at the right moment. And she was, as her children knew well, queen of the right moment, well capable of calling a halt while leaving Mr Doyle with the impression that he was the one who had made the decision to stop. But she was relieved to see him so absorbed, so much his old indefatigable self that she decided not to interfere. The laurels would grow again and if they didn't, what of it.

'I'm expecting Eugene to ring about Sunday, to say for sure ...' she said, looking over at Mr Doyle who listened by default, too exhausted to pick up the newspaper.

'Didn't he tell you he was coming already?' Mr Doyle tapped the arm of his chair rhythmically, a countdown routine, creating a sense of urgency to force the information he was searching for to the surface. When it did emerge he grasped it like a swooping gull and blurted it out immediately.

'He told you he was coming. He did. I heard him myself. Here. Last Sunday.'

Mr Doyle had come to life again, his face meat red in the kitchen heat, mildly pulsating after his afternoon's work in the garden.

He found himself unexpectedly content, looking forward to Sunday with Eugene, as well as the regulars – the boys and their families – all coming for dinner at The Acre. Before that, Saturday, a day that still held all its old excitement.

'I'll set out good and early for the meat in the morning.' His voice was full of resolution, charged with that spirit of boyish co-operation, well intentioned but inclined to make Mrs Doyle uneasy. Still she would have readily admitted that anything was better than the tetchiness and that loose-end presence about the house which made it almost impossible for her to get on with her day's work.

'If you think there's a doubt about him coming, I'll give him a ring tomorrow.'

'Ah no, I remember now, you're right.' Mrs Doyle's voice was slack, all the earlier concern gone out of it.

It didn't seem to occur to Mr Doyle that her doubt about Eugene coming to dinner on Sunday was a pretence from the start, a ploy to stop him from slipping into a downward spiral. She was familiar with the symptoms, his impatience, his way of casting about as though he were in a room he'd never been in before, the aggressive way he kept clearing his throat. Guiding him to an even keel was something she did without giving it much thought. The approach had to be indirect otherwise he would become defensive. She could never have said, 'Now cheer up, tomorrow is Saturday – the Club, remember? And then there's Sunday ...' He would have interrupted as soon as he heard the words cheer up.

'There's nothing the matter with me. I don't know where you got that notion from.'

He would then claim that he had been misread, was always

being misread, and from there on in it was downhill until he reached his favourite perch – indignation.

Mrs Doyle's strategy was based on a very particular view of the circumstances under which people lose the run of themselves. She saw every individual as a living battlefield in which their better instincts were permanently under attack from their base instincts. It was not so much a theory as a graphic picture. Good – conspiratorial and wise – gently guiding one arm and Evil – vexed and cunning – maniacally clutching the other. If the evil side suspected a new offensive by the good then it became more wily. Good had to be very subtle, tiptoeing around the individual with its noble intentions well disguised.

When she looked at Mr Doyle, exhausted after his day at the laurels, Mrs Doyle saw a man whose defences were down, a man who could not be alert to the forces that were working on his exhaustion, determined to turn it into bad form and ill will. Her job was to intervene, to turn his attention – subtly – to the good things to come, Saturday night in the Club, Sunday dinner with the family and lots more besides. That was the spirit in which she set out to coax his better side to the fore. And while she might raise her eyes and laugh whenever Mr Doyle called her his better half, it was a title she worked hard to earn and rightfully deserved.

At times she did become exasperated. All the more so since Eve left. Despite all Eve's talk about exploitation, Mrs Doyle saw her as an ally in the battle to keep everyone happy.

Whenever Eve called her a slave, which she often did, Mrs Doyle brushed the accusation aside, sometimes with perky good humour, sometimes with a 'that's-the-way-of-the-world' type remark. She had dozens of these and delivered them all with the same air of mock resignation. She regarded Eve's talk of exploitation and slavery as a part of the phase she was going through and went along with it to a point, but she herself had a definite policy of being content with her lot and by and large that ruled out looking critically at it.

'There's a difference between slavery and not putting yourself first all the time, a big difference,' she'd told Eve once. 'It might look like slavery to you but you'd be surprised. When it comes down to it, people respect you because they know that you're not putting yourself first.'

'You mean that self-sacrifice gets you places,' Eve said, irritated by the very mention of the word 'respect'.

'That's not what I meant.'

'Well that's what it sounded like to me.'

'It's to do with respect ...' Mrs Doyle said with faltering authority. But in her attempt to explain why, she got confused, wrapping it all up with a nod and 'you know well what I mean'.

It was clear to Eve that Mrs Doyle felt compromised by having to defend herself in this way. It was as if she knew that what she was saying was foolish, that she was leaving herself open to ridicule. Uneasy about how defenceless her mother appeared – and aware of how keenly she felt her lack of formal education – Eve held back, giving her a chance to recoup.

'I'm just telling you the way things work,' Mrs Doyle said, relieved to be reunited with her practical self. She was soon telling Eve that, in time, she would come around to her way of thinking. Eve despaired of ever getting her mother to take a real look at her situation and just let her rattle on. Mrs Doyle eventually brought the conversation – a monologue by that stage – to what she considered a satisfactory close, asking Eve in a very reasonable voice, 'What on earth is wrong with a woman taking responsibility for peace and harmony in her own home?'

'Nothing,' Eve said blithely, her sights firmly fixed on a future in which she hoped such a question would cause embarrassment if not rage.

Eve's brothers understood very well how she felt but they considered her challenges – 'She's not your slave, you know,' – feeble and mimicked her in a skittish nasal monotone. If she tried to get her mother to assist her against them, Mrs Doyle was likely to tell her to ignore them. Or worse, much worse, 'Offer it up.' Eve particularly disliked the notion of offering things up. But, like a lot of the catch-cries that go unquestioned in childhood, it occasionally rang in her ears, presenting itself as a way of enduring hardship.

Though long since detached from its original religious roots it was a philosophy which had continued to serve Mrs Doyle well. But as the winter approached and with it long days alone with Mr Doyle she began to think that there was a limit to what she could offer up. The swallowing duct, like a vacuum cleaner hose, could get clogged if it was used as indiscriminately and as often as she sensed she was going to have to use it.

She was aware well in advance of the changes that were about to take place in her world and understood for the most part the impact they would have. She knew she would miss Eve – her 'late lamb', a name she still occasionally used despite Eve's attempts to ban it. She knew only too well that it would not be plain sailing with Mr Doyle about the place all day. Also, out there somewhere was Noel, refusing to come to The Acre unless he could bring his new family. But she was used to fitting her own day-to-day life into the margins of those lives around her and so she confidently set out to adjust her routine to suit her new situation.

In some ways Eve admired her mother, how resourceful she was, the way she just ploughed on and she would have liked to talk about the future but almost everything Mrs Doyle said had a God-be-between-us-and-all-harm tone to it which allowed Eve to do little more than listen and agree.

As it turned out Mrs Doyle's new routine worked well enough. But there were black spots – times when her policy of being content with her lot failed to keep gloomy thoughts at bay.

As she spread Mr Doyle's Committee Member's blazer on the bed, such thoughts were not very far away. Running her finger along the razor sharp crease of his flannels, she began to go through in her mind the people she hoped would be at the club that evening. It was hard to believe that it was months and not decades since, complete with photographs of their cruise and a selection of exotic liqueurs, they had bounced into the club like teenagers.

The yacht club was a wooden colonial style building situated in the old harbour, right down at the water's edge. From the bay on Saturday nights it looked like a Mississippi showboat – its lemon and orange lights sizzling on the lapping water. There was nothing glitzy about the interior, though, with its oak panelling, pipe-smoke fug and pools of soft muted light spreading from the large tasselled red shades.

Members frequently boasted that the waiting list was longer than the actual list of members. Mr Doyle, through a senior colleague at Good, Good and Stavely, had been accepted when he was still only an administrative assistant. The company had a connection with the club which dated back to the early nineteenth century when the head of the Good family, Harold Good, himself an enthusiastic yachtsman, gave the building to the newly formed club. The details of this connection emerged during the course of Mr Doyle's research into the history of the club, a task he undertook in the months leading up to the cruise he and Mrs Doyle went on following his retirement.

He had begun corresponding with yacht clubs in all the ports of call on the cruise itinerary. The possibility of twinning with his own club, although mooted in all the letters he sent, was only taken up by one of them. The Wanchai Club in Hong Kong. When all the groundwork was done, Mr Doyle presented the project to the other committee members. Their club had been, as Mr Doyle put it, 'selected for this honour by one of the most prestigious yacht clubs in the world'.

When he and Mrs Doyle arrived in Hong Kong they were surprised to find that the Wanchai Club was located on the thirty-sixth floor of a building in a busy business district of the city. Eventually they found their way to a low-ceilinged, but unexpectedly large room – which clearly, from the array of plaques on the door, served as headquarters of several water sports clubs.

The twinning ceremony turned out to be the high point of the whole cruise. Coats of arms were officially swapped and the president of The Wanchai Yacht Club, Mr Han Lee, gave a short speech welcoming the Doyles to Hong Kong. Members of each club were declared members of the other. Mrs Doyle sat to the right of the podium, unsure if the woman sitting on the chair beside her was Mr Han Lee's wife or not. This she planned to find out – discreetly – when Mr Han Lee's speech was over. But before he left the podium a large ghetto blaster was produced and while everyone was still silent Mr Han Lee pressed the 'play' button. The recording – 'God Save the Queen' – was old and the closing bars were drowned out by the Pathe News screen music, giving the impression that the whole tape was recorded in a cinema. Everyone stood up, many bowing in the Doyles' direction as they did.

After lunch midst apologetic stop-start laughter, the sort in which misunderstandings get unravelled, it emerged that Mr Han Lee was unsure of what Mrs Doyle's connection with Mr Doyle was. She had not been mentioned in any of the correspondence and although ostentatiously welcomed, she had not, in fact, been expected at the ceremony. Mr Doyle had assumed that because they were together everyone would automatically know who she was. But sensitive to the many different arrangements people have with each other Mr Han Lee avoided introducing his own wife in case it might embarrass Mr Doyle. It all ended in a cacophony of titters and guffaws.

The photographs of the cruise – all one hundred and forty – were arranged in sequence by Mrs Doyle in an album with a white embossed velveteen cover. Mr Doyle called it the wedding album. As it was being passed around their friends at the club, he joked about their second honeymoon, telling them that he was in too much of a rush to enjoy the first one.

As each page of the album was turned he found something new to joke about.

'See this one,' he said, pointing to an over exposed photograph of Mrs Doyle, 'I don't know how many different angles I tried before she was satisfied that her stretch marks wouldn't be recorded for the world to behold.'

The group bunched in to look at the photograph of Mrs Doyle on a reclining sun chair, curled up like a cat.

One couple, first timers in the club, guests of friends of the Doyles, glanced at Mrs Doyle, wondering if she was offended. But even before she spoke it was clear from her expression, a cocktail of guile and glee, that she didn't mind being teased in this way and could give as good as she got.

'On the second day of cruise His Nib's sunglasses fell into the sea. The Mediterranean,' she added as she drew attention to Mr Doyle's squint in a series of photographs on the same page.

'Surely you could have bought a new pair, probably even duty free,' Leo Hanlon said, looking absent-mindedly at a photograph of a weary Mr Doyle on his way up to the Acropolis.

Placing her hand on Leo Hanlon's upper arm Mrs Doyle gently pushed him away.

'You must be joking, I had a difficult enough time persuading him not to ask the captain to stop the ship.'

As the group laughed Mrs Doyle displayed the large topaz Mr Doyle had bought for her in Santorini, turning the album pages until she found the photograph the jeweller had taken of them, their arms draped lazily over each other's shoulders.

'Mind you, the insurance costs more than the ring itself. Just goes to show what good value it was. And to think I had to spend half the morning looking at it before he took out his wallet.'

Almost everybody enjoyed their affectionate banter. But there were a few couples who, when the laughter died away, felt that their lot didn't measure up. The Muldoons, for instance, a quiet complicitious couple, rarely left without Mrs Muldoon having what Mr Muldoon called 'a puss on'. But if the Doyles had ever suspected that the way they went on unsettled others they would have been much more restrained. They didn't like to think of themselves as unkind – quite the contrary – their generosity to others was a secret they shared, a secret they would never disclose because it would seem like bragging.

The person who enjoyed that generosity most was Eugene Wall, a regular at the Doyles' for over a decade. 'One of our own,' Mrs Doyle would say. He and Noel were the best of pals in secondary school. They were part of a big gang, who, as children had been to the same pass-the-parcel and chocolate rice krispies birthday parties, the same tennis hops in their early teens and later the same pub. In that way it followed that a girlfriend – Eve – or a boyfriend – Eugene – selected from within the group were more welcome than those brought in from the world at large.

Eugene's visits to the Doyles were no less frequent after Eve left for Raleigh Reilly than they had been before. He just sauntered in and took his place among them, slumping into a chair to watch TV, half-heartedly protesting if asked to stay for whatever meal was on the way and there was always a meal on the way at the Doyles'. But on those Sundays when he was formally invited, he came to the hall door, all dressed up and if it was answered by Mr Doyle, as it usually was at lunch time on Sundays, Eugene held his hand out like a salesman, delighting Mr Doyle with his enthusiasm.

His arrival on the Sunday following the mix-up about whether or not he had been invited was no different. He stood there, beaming and slightly glossy, his hand ready as always to clasp Mr Doyle's.

'Come in. Come in,' Mr Doyle said. And then much faster, 'Come in. Come in. Come in.'

Mr Doyle, unused to the idea that people might like to decide for themselves, had already poured sherry into six ornately cut glasses, all clustered together on a small black tray he and Mrs Doyle had bought in Sorrento.

'Here. Sit down. Sit down. The others will be here soon. Sit down. By the way – one thing – before they come, Yvonne's room, I'm going to redecorate it, it's a sort of surprise for when she comes home at Christmas. I thought I'd ask your advice about one of those new jazzy shops. If you had a half an hour to spare at lunch time – next week some day.'

Eugene nodded, his glass close to his lips, waiting for an opportunity to sip.

'We might have a bite to eat beforehand.' Mr Doyle studied Eugene's reaction carefully as he spoke. 'It's the wallpaper that's the problem. Whatever I picked, bound to be wrong. You'd know what to pick. Something mod.'

Several times that afternoon Mr Doyle took Eugene aside – a new concern, a new question, some complication or other. Eugene had all the answers and by the time he was ready to leave he found himself more or less in charge of redecorating Eve's room.

As he waved goodbye Mr Doyle tried not to congratulate himself on his success, but his satisfaction was so deep-seated that he only managed to hold back a broad beam of a smile until Eugene was out of sight.

Chapter

5

EVE SAT IN THE lobby of the Elbar Security Company, fifteen minutes early for her interview. She kept the palm of her hand pressed against the envelope in her pocket. Official confirmation. Student at Raleigh Reilly, Interdisciplinary MA – Behavioral Sciences. Some people from her motivation theory tutorial had been working part-time with Elbar since term began.

'Yvonne, Mr Hollenheimer will see you now.' The voice on the PA system resounded around the lobby. Gave the impression that there was a great big dome overhead. Eve glanced at the other people around. Mustn't apologise, she told herself. Just go. What's it to them?

'Hi. Larry Hollenheimer. Psychological Services. Larry.'

There was a sweet cosmetic smell in his office. Familiar. Maybe lavender talcum powder, Eve thought as she approached Larry. But it grew faint, giving way to a leathery smell. Shoe shop, a bit intoxicating. Made her draw back a little as she shook hands.

'If you were me,' Larry said in a slow, evenly paced voice, 'what would you ask you' – pointing at Eve – 'about yourself?'

Immediately Eve thought of her mother trying to help her

with maths homework. 'It's a trick question,' Mrs Doyle would say as though that in itself was the answer.

'I don't know. I think I'd ask me, the person sitting here,' Eve said, pointing at herself, 'if they were good at trick questions.'

Larry wagged his finger from side to side as if he was demonstrating the action of a windscreen wiper. 'Very good. Now what we have to ask next is ...' and he began using both hands, drawing Eve forward, encouraging her to anticipate the question. Then one of his phones burred, piping intermittently before the pips, rising in volume, merged into a continuous piercing sound. Important. He picked up the receiver and immediately covered the mouthpiece with his hand.

'The first briefing session is on Friday. Can you make it?'

Eve nodded vigorously and whispered, 'What time?'

'Two.'

'Fine. Bye.'

Eve breezed through the lobby – an ice skater leaving the rink after a lap of honour.

The project, which Larry introduced at the Friday briefing session as P. S. I Love You, had been in operation for over six months and was in such demand that Elbar had decided to form a number of other teams offering the same service.

The style of presentation of the P. S. I love you project was relaxed. Chirpy banter between Larry and Abe Shamone, the co-ordinator, while they put screens, monitors and revolving charts in place. Soon Eve and the other members of the team were watching a video. A woman, mid to late thirties in a loose floral dress was taping a notice to the close-meshed wire fence surrounding a children's playground.

Zoom in on the notice. A photograph. Girl aged about seven, ordinary, innocent looking, chubby-cheeked. There were four or five lines typed underneath but it was not possible to read them.

An unidentified off-screen voice, it could have been a casual passer by, asked, 'What are you doing?'

The woman in the floral dress, cordial but sad looking, turned and did not answer until her face fully filled the frame. 'This is a picture of my daughter. Naomi. Naomi was abducted outside our home eleven weeks ago.'

Faintly in the background is the be-bop build-up to the coast-to-coast hit, 'Have you seen her?'

Zoom in on the photograph of Naomi. A liquid, looked like a mixture of sealing wax and blood, dripped on to it forming the word ABDUCTED.

Zoom out, gradually revealing dozens of other similar photographs, all stamped ABDUCTED.

Abe pointed the zapper at the monitor, freezing the frame.

'There's a whole lot of worried people out there. Worried people who need our help.' Deep furrows appeared on Abe's forehead and he shook his head gravely. 'And that's where P. S. I love you started from. Helping People. It started because Elbar wanted to help people like Naomi's mom and it continues because . . .' he paused as a kindergarten teacher might, allowing the class to finish the sentence' . . . because . . .'

'Elbar wants to go on helping people,' someone behind her said, surprising Eve who was still looking at all the little faces stamped ABDUCTED.

Larry, large and avuncular, smiled as he surveyed the newly assembled team.

'We fail our children,' he said, cradling his hands as though he were holding something very precious, 'through our ignorance. We think that by telling them about bad people we are somehow saving them from the clutches of such people.' Suddenly he became a zealot, his eyes startling as he braced himself for what Eve sensed was going to be a key concept. 'Telling is not protecting.' He stood, momentarily drained by the delivery. He turned away from the group for a few seconds letting it sink in. When he turned back, he had assumed a different guise, awkward, a little embarrassed that he should be the medium through which such a remarkable truth had passed.

'Children,' he explained, 'are unable to grasp an abstraction such as bad people. What's a bad person to them? Someone who takes their candy? Someone who looks scary? These are bad people.' He looked at each member of the group in turn extending the word 'bad' until Eve began to think that it was an attempt at humour, a sheep bleat which would, in some way or other, become relevant to the point he was making.

'Children need things to be tangible. They've got to be able to hook in and that's what P. S. I love you guarantees. It provides them with a simulated abduction experience.' He thrust his hands, fingers splayed, towards the group, resting his case. 'But for them of course it's the real thing, they are getting the concrete experience they need in order to learn how to handle an abductor. Therapy and tuition in contra tactics follow directly, but you,' he said dismissively, 'won't be involved at that end of things. Any questions?' Larry asked, nodding to Abe who held the zapper like a hand gun, pointing it directly at the monitor where the abducted children waited to be banished from the screen.

A step by step explanation of the P. S. I love you package followed, beginning with a client profile. 'They are,' the soft undulating voice stated, 'a couple in their late thirties, upper socio-economic grouping but rarely above the ninetieth percentile.'

'People in that bracket usually have their own security personnel,' Abe interjected and he was about to say something else when the video voice continued, 'let's take a look at their home'.

Through the branches of a copper beech the camera stole up on a classic clapboard house. A boy in a check shirt and jeans raked leaves into little piles on a tightly mowed lawn. The piano music which had been rambling aimlessly, plunged into discord as the camera picked out a window. Inside, a girl aged about nine, pig-tails and freckles, was emptying cake mixture into a tin, supervised by her relaxed smiling mother. They wore matching aprons.

'The majority of people availing of the P. S. I love you programme know or know of someone who has been the victim of an abduction,' a new voice announced. The tone was authoritative but not assertive, a little like that of a newsreader.

'That includes attempted abduction,' Abe interjected again.

Larry nodded conspicuously.

What was it about men, Eve wondered, that made them behave like that.

A sequence followed in which the woman previously seen baking with the little girl arrived at Elbar Securities with a man, her husband. His arm protectively around her shoulder, they rushed up the steps as though they were being followed by reporters – a tiny anti-climatic moment, a false note of fear, re-enforced by a change in the music, one of those Gershwin pieces which builds up a sense of expectation of what is to follow only to curve and skid into something unanticipated.

The couple are seen as part of a group of other couples.

'The prospective clients,' the voice continued, 'present the team with a profile of their child.' Larry and Abe, members of the original P. S. I love you team, momentarily appeared on the screen. Both leaned forward to see themselves better but the cameras moved back to the prospective clients and Larry and Abe lost interest, leaning back in their seats which squeaked in unison.

'The profile the parents present of their child is very important.' A short clip of the little girl turning out the cake mixture followed. 'We need to know how the child will react when he or she is abducted. If they are prone to extreme reactions or have any type of neurological disorder we advise the parents not to go ahead. But if,' and here the voice became suffused with compassion, 'in such an instance the clients make a particularly good case then we can adapt the package to suit their requirements.'

The couple on the screen kept interrupting each other, not so much to dispute the details of the profile they were presenting of their daughter, Mitsy, but to verify what the other was saying.

When Mitsy was seen on the screen she was cycling along a spotlessly clean tree-lined avenue singing 'I Got a House in Baltimore, little Liza Jane'. In the distance, two boys were skateboarding up and down a make-shift ramp. The background piano tinkling subtly gave way to a rustling sound, something moving through an unseen undergrowth and then twigs breaking under a heavy footstep.

An unidentified male voice said, 'Hi. You must be Mitsy Bell. I'm Curt Mulloy. I work with your dad at Oskil Tucker. You've probably heard him talk about me. Curt Mulloy?' No gap to let the question sink in. 'I've got good news for you, he's just been promoted to vice president of the company. Aren't you proud?' Again no gap. 'Right now he is planning a celebration. He wants you and your mom and your brother William to be there. Asked me if I'd come out and collect you. Hop in and we'll go and collect your mom and William.'

'What about my bike?'

'Oh leave that there, it'll be safe. You'll be back in a couple of hours. Your dad has told me all about you, about how well you look after those hamsters of yours. Can't recall their names right now . . .'

'Ike and Theodore.'

'Right. I remember now, called after two famous presidents . . . Oh. Look at that. We're practically out of gas. We're going to have to get to a filling station before we go to collect your mom and William. Can you tell me how to get to the nearest one?'

'We can go back to my house and all go to Dad's office in my mom's car.' The music stopped and a close up of a stubbly

Adam's apple going up and down filled the screen.

'That way I'd have to leave my car at your house and come back with you later to collect it. That wouldn't be very smart, now would it? And besides, you guys wouldn't get to drive home together 'cos there'd be two cars and that would be a disappointment for your dad – and we don't want to disappoint him on the day he's been made vice president of Oskil Tucker. Do we? Now let me see. I think I saw a gas station at the exit for Cricketgrove County.'

'I'm tired and I'm not feeling too good,' Mitsy drawled as they sat waiting for the attendant to fill the tank.

A fat hand with rectangular tufts of black hair between the finger joints dug deep into a pocket, rooting for loose change.

'Here, how about you go get yourself a Coke.'

As Mitsy skipped over to the gas station store the fat hand began making elaborate signals to a person sitting in the driver seat of a wine coloured Oldsmobile near the car wash depot. A slender white hand, viewed in the side mirror of the Oldsmobile, responded with a single firm gesture. With that the fat hand hurriedly paid the pump attendant, swung the steering wheel almost full circle and within seconds the car was tearing down the highway.

When Mitsy came out of the store her mother was waiting with a happy-ending expression and, after what appeared like a calm discussion, the pair made their way over to the Oldsmobile and drove to the Elbar Security building where a team, which included Abe and Larry, were 'on hand to develop the experience and so elicit the child's natural self-protective impulses'.

'Any questions?' Abe asked, standing up and stretching his arms until he looked like a boy poised to play airoplane raids.

Eve had reservations but they were intuitive. Her attempt to frame them into a coherent question was foiled by a very graphic memory, Eve aged about seven, running down a sloping field. She tried to remember where the field was, but couldn't, and gave up trying, disorientated by the thought that there were parts of her own life that were out of reach.

'Looks to me like this is all about scaring kids,' a middle aged woman at the back of the room said. Eve turned around, nodding in agreement. The woman was sitting beside the door, well away from the others. She had two bags of groceries at her feet. Eve figured she must have arrived late for the briefing session.

Larry congratulated the woman on the pertinence of her question and smiled warmly in her direction. 'Fear is one of our most valuable defences, one which, if handled properly, will serve us well. But it can also destroy us so we must try to control it and use it cautiously. May I ask you a personal question?'

The woman threw her right hand upwards, opening it loosely.

'Sure, go right ahead.'

'Have you been inoculated against any potentially fatal diseases?'

'I have. Hasn't everyone?' She looked at the group. Eve tried to appear supportive but was unaware of the direction the conversation was taking.

'Yes, everyone has,' Larry said, pausing like a lawyer. 'And you all know how inoculation works? Right?' He began to pace up and down in front of the monitor. 'A minute quantity of the life-threatening virus is injected into your system which, registering the threat, manufactures the antibodies necessary to keep you safe from that virus for life. Well that's exactly how the P. S. I love you package operates. A controlled abduction experience becomes the foundation on which life-long resistance to abduction is built.'

'I guess if you look at it that way ...' the woman said, dawdling on the word 'way'.

Overwhelmed by how much sense it all made, Eve lost sight of her initial reservations. 'It's only a question of time,' Larry said, in a matter-of-fact way, 'before simulated abduction becomes as routine a part of growing up as losing your baby teeth.'

The more Eve thought about it the more convinced she became of its brilliance. There was, she told Star that night, 'something especially fulfilling about protecting children'.

'Sounds a bit spooky to me,' Star said, 'but at a hundred bucks a scoop I could get over that.'

Eve wondered how Star was always able to be so clear about how she felt about things, apparently without giving them any thought at all. The instant she told Eve what she thought about the P. S. I love you programme, Eve got the idea that in fact she felt the exact same way. A bit spooky but worth the money. Very straightforward. But for reasons she had not, until then, looked at very closely she needed to convince herself that by getting involved she was first and foremost helping others.

Eve looked out of the big window, vaguely noticing a ripple in the glass but not seeing anything in particular. She did not at that moment make what she would many years later claim was a life decision. But she had unwittingly crossed a threshold into a world where she would, as a point of principle, habitually take stock of her own responses, examining them to see to how they were at odds with what she really felt.

Star, who had always assumed that what people said reflected exactly what they thought, did not notice any change in Eve. But it was apparent almost straight away to Irma Knoll, Equality Studies Registrar. Eve was, she pointed out to the Department Co-ordinator, Nancy Alldice, 'emerging from some sort of chrysalis'.

Suddenly Eve was the focus of both Irma's and Nancy's attention, a student whom they recognised as 'very rapidly finding her voice' – a development they attributed directly to her participation in the Cross Cultural Study of Women's Experience.

'It would,' Irma suggested, 'be appropriate to tell her how

well she's doing on the basis that confidence may have been an inhibiting factor at the outset.'

When, after a tutorial in late November, Irma told Eve that Nancy whom Eve had only met briefly, wished to see her, Eve immediately assumed that there was something wrong; her contributions to the course were inadequate, irrelevant, her questions were not searching enough. She had no difficulty in coming up with a list of possibilities.

Eve's notion of a head of an Equality Studies department was so different to the type of person Nancy Alldice turned out to be that when she walked into her office she felt like apologising.

'Please sit down, Eve.'

Nancy Alldice was quietly spoken and so at ease that Eve, who might well have sat on the edge of the chair, sat right back, letting both her arms fall to the side.

'Irma has told me how well you're doing on the Comparative programme ...' she paused and Eve looked at her apprehensively expecting her to say 'but'.

'Your progress has been very impressive and we thought you should know that.'

Eve shifted a little in the chair, struggling against an impulse to say something self-deprecatory, and so much effort went into that struggle that her response was limited to a series of quick nods. But Nancy Alldice was well practised at putting students at their ease.

'It's very gratifying for us to observe your progress. The course is very much at the experimental stage and I think you probably know that it's not without its critics here on campus.'

'Thank you,' Eve said, feeling that there was something brazen about accepting a compliment so unreservedly. Questions like, would Nancy Alldice think she had a tip about herself?, were all too ready to form, but Eve held out, determined to take her place in a world where there was no place for false modesty.

'Thank you,' she said again, this time in an accent similar to

Nancy's, which to Eve seemed without nuance or innuendo.

'The Comparative Study has had its difficulties. The amount of the group's time Elizabeth and Haley have been demanding – I've spoken to Elizabeth and she has agreed to talk to Haley about it. The original arrangement was that Haley should attend on her own.'

'Oh I don't mind. It's fine about them,' Eve said in a great rush.

'You're probably aware of how things are for them.'

Eve looked at Nancy, trying to figure out if she was asking her a question. It was difficult to tell.

'They've made no headway. Their perception of their relationship is no different now that it was when they arrived here eighteen months ago. I have to admit that I was over optimistic about their chances of finding lives that were less intensely dependent on each other.'

'What happened to them?' Eve asked, swept along by Nancy's deeply felt concern for Elizabeth and Haley.

'Oh nothing happened to them. It's not a trauma-related condition. It's just an extreme case of a mother and daughter sharing the same psychic space.'

As Eve began to apply the diagnosis to Elizabeth and Haley's relationship she repeated the words 'the same psychic space', giving Nancy the impression that she had not understood the implications of the condition.

'At a very elementary level it means that when, for instance, Haley is in good shape, you know, happily getting on with things, Elizabeth goes into a downward swing. She feels vulnerable, isolated, redundant. Of course it works the other way around too. When Elizabeth ...' and here Nancy paused to draw breath and as she did she realised that she need not go any further with the explanation. 'We thought that it was a classic case of Psychological Siamese Twins and all we had to do was get them involved in a separation programme. From the start Irma, who was monitoring the programme, pointed out that it was a Yin Yan relationship. They were psycho-logically Siamese all right but unfortunately the sort where separation means the demise of one of them.'

Given free range, Nancy's compassion was rapidly giving way to conviction. But Eve appeared so spellbound that Nancy became uncharacteristically self-conscious and smiled reassuringly.

'I'm not sure what the outcome will be. Whatever it is they can't be permitted to continue dominating the Comparative tutorials.'

Eve was intrigued by the idea of mothers and daughters sharing the same psychic space and in the weeks that followed she came to believe that all mothers and daughters were, to a greater or lesser extent faced with the same problem. Before long the theory began to play a part in her ongoing plans to ensure that her own life would not turn out like her mother's.

Chapter

6

DESIRÉ GOOD, WITH thirty-five years service on the steering committee for the Good, Good and Stavely Christmas party, was by far the longest serving member. She always opened the preliminary mid November meeting by recounting her first memory of that party in the billiard room at Innisbreige, her old family home. No one smoked as nostalgically as Desiré Good. Year in year out, newly elected committee members watched her hold a cigarette between her skeletal fingers and draw memories from it with a sinewy intensity that kept her the focus of everyone's attention. But only for that first meeting. When it became known, as it did very rapidly, that she wanted to have the Christmas party in Innisbreige, a large dilapidated grade C guest house, she was unceremoniously marginalised. She bore her fate with dignity, a position she hoped would earn her the sort of respect her family had enjoyed down the years.

Mr Doyle had always disliked her. He hated her hair nets and cavalry twill slacks. He had tried to have her banned from the lobby where she had a knack of appearing anytime he passed through with a client. She should, he tried to persuade his fellow board members, be confined to the basement where the company archive was located, arguing that she was lucky to be there at all. No other insurance company had an archivist. It was an embarrassment.

She was not – as many Good, Good and Stavely secretaries claimed – hurt by the offhand way Mr Doyle and some other senior managers treated her. She was protected by the belief that she was paying the price of being the last surviving Good. Her father had had to deal with some pretty rough types in his day. Now it was her turn and she welcomed the opportunity to display some of the Good mettle that had made the company what it was.

She volunteered, as she did every year, to keep the minutes of the Christmas party steering committee meeting. In addition, she agreed to look after the pensioners on the night – make sure they were all invited, organise transport for them and in general see to it that they had an enjoyable night. She knew them all. Their careers, for the most part, had straddled her own at Good, Good and Stavely and to many of them she had remained Miss Good, a reminder that the company was built on a solid foundation.

She set about her task by contacting the recently retired members of staff first. Top of the list sent to her by the personnel department was Mr Doyle.

The Doyles were counting the days until Eve came home for Christmas. The redecoration of her room had taken Mr Doyle and Eugene much longer than they first thought. The ceiling paper was the main problem. Mr Doyle was hard-pushed not to bark at Eugene when an entire freshly pasted strip peeled off, folding and crumpling as they both tried to stop it from hitting the ground. Mr Doyle was quick to see that involving Eugene might backfire if there was another episode like that so he hired a decorator to complete what remained of the job.

By early December, the Doyles had plans in place for almost every one of Eve's twelve days at home. But, anxious not to overdo the planning, they organised all the family get-togethers for the middle of the day, lunch at Anton's, lunch at

Syl's, lunch at Aunt Mona's and the annual family lunch at the club. In that way Eve would be free to go out in the evenings with Eugene. They congratulated each other on this arrangement at every turn, each time reiterating their agreement that Christmas dinner at The Acre would be at the usual mid-afternoon time. Eugene would come afterwards to spend the evening – they didn't have to invite him.

Mr Doyle secretly organised third party insurance cover for Eugene on Mrs Doyle's Mini. The kind of pleasure he got from behind-the-scenes ploys like that was immense. It was wholly personal, a roguish delight in having a trick up his sleeve. The person who was most surprised whenever one of these tricks was revealed was Mrs Doyle. She regarded secrecy as a strength and all the more so because it was one she did not have herself.

During the weeks of non-stop preparation in early December Mr Doyle was in singularly good form. There was so much to be done. He spent most of those mornings on the phone, ordering spiced beef, smoked salmon, Stilton. He rang every wine merchant in the city searching for a Portuguese wine he had seen recommended in the Grapevine column in the *Examiner*. Only once did he lose the run of himself and even that might have been avoided had Mrs Doyle been there. The run up to Christmas was hectic at the meals-on-wheels centre and she did not arrive home that day until the late afternoon.

Before she got out of her car she sensed there was something wrong and she sat, both hands on the steering wheel, examining the house, searching for a possible source of her premonition. Several things crossed her mind, all of them familiar – the death of one of her children, of Mr Doyle, illness. Imagining the worst was her way of keeping it at bay. As a consequence she handled lesser misfortunes, sprains and grazes, disappointment and upsets with calm competence.

'That shrunken busybody was on again,' Mr Doyle blurted out before she had taken the key out of the door.

She took off her gloves and put them into her coat pocket,

knowing full well that he would not even wait for her to ask before speaking again.

'Desiré Good,' he neighed with frustration. 'I told her the party was on the same night as Yvonne was due in. She refused point blank to change it. I rang Thornley. He wasn't prepared to go over the head of the organising committee. A leopard never changes his spots. So no office party. A fine thank-you.'

By the time he had finished speaking Mrs Doyle had filled a sherry glass to the very brim, offering it to him as she set about thinking of a way around the problem.

At first it seemed insurmountable, but after about an hour, with Mrs Doyle sifting through the facts, a compromise began to emerge. But it didn't take on a definite shape until much later – until she felt he was ready to accept it.

Eugene became a key player in the new arrangement, more than willing to drive Mr Doyle to the Good, Good and Stavely Christmas party at eight, head on to the airport and wait until Eve's flight arrived in at ten and then pick up Mr Doyle on the way back to The Acre where Mrs Doyle would be waiting with a trolley supper and a roaring fire.

The following week Desiré Good rang to enquire if Mr Doyle – Dick as she always called him – 'had managed to sort out his tizzy about the date of the party'.

'Why are you whispering?' she asked Mrs Doyle in a loud voice. 'Is there someone asleep? Is Dick napping? Oh the luxury of it, the bliss of retirement. Divine.'

Mrs Doyle looked over at Mr Doyle's newspaper, held like a riot shield in front of him, hoping he wouldn't ask who was on the phone.

'Shan't delay you a jiff. Just one thing. This year's theme, can't remember if I told Dick or not. Cowboys and Indians. It needn't be anything elaborate, just to get a party spirit going.'

'Cowboys and Indians,' Mrs Doyle repeated.

'That's it,' Desiré Good replied, pleased to display her ability to keep up with the changing times. Mrs Doyle eventually managed a hesitant yes, which Desiré Good, followed with a speedy 'Cheerypip'.

Mr Doyle didn't want to be the odd man out, but neither did he want to wear the big flying saucer of a sombrero he and Mrs Doyle had brought back from Malaga. And the yellow and red checkered head scarf Mrs Doyle produced as a possible necktie was, he insisted, out of the question altogether. Still she persuaded him to bring both along on the night. Just in case.

Gathering himself to get out of the car and make a dash for the hotel in the pouring rain he spotted three former colleagues, Bill Cass, Terry Spillane and Andy Shaw strutting into the hotel lobby wearing cowboy boots and Stetsons. In a great rush, clutching the rear view mirror and twisting it violently, he put on the checkered scarf, knotting it tightly to one side of his neck. It was not possible to put the sombrero on until he got out of the car.

As Eugene moved off, shouting goodbye through the steamy car windows, he found himself thinking how much he liked and admired Mr Doyle. And Mrs Doyle. All the Doyles. Eve. Three postcards. The thought had a way of hurtling itself into his line of vision despite the countless strategies he had developed to keep it as far away as possible. He rolled his lips in anticipation of the pint he could already visualise, sitting on one of the low black tables in the airport lounge. In two hours, he thought to himself, Eve would be there, standing in front of him explaining why she had not written more often. No point in thinking about it in advance.

In the airport bar he whiled away the time trying to imagine how Eve might have changed. There were lots of couples, he told himself, happily married with three or four children who hadn't known one another as long as he and Eve had.

Each pint tasted better than the one before, spawning feelings of such closeness that he bought Eve a drink. A lager and lime. 'Just like old times,' he whispered as he placed it next to his pint, admiring how well the two drunks looked together.

Even if he was drunk, which he wasn't, he would not have heard the announcement in the airport lounge. There was so much pouring out of the PA system, such a clamour in the lounge, that a single announcement alerting people to a delay in an incoming flight from New York could easily have gone unheard.

When the announcement was repeated Eugene was pre-occupied, bobbing up and down in the crowd in the arrivals hall, making sure he saw everyone who filed through the gates. He had began to panic, uncertain if he was going to recognise Eve when she came through. He looked for her in everyone, increasingly unsure of what she looked like. He stared for so long at one woman that she smiled, faintly, convinced by the concentrated way he examined her that she must know him from somewhere. Then, as though preceded by an instant of absolute silence the announcement flooded the whole build-ing, filling Eugene, to his own surprise, with relief. He had little time to think about why because in that instant he was seized by an overwhelming need to urinate.

Whatever was going to happen to him next wasn't going to happen in the toilets which gave him a sense of security. He often took refuge in toilets, disappearing from crowded noisy places in an effort to become reunited with himself. In the futuristic anonymity of the white ceramic glare he began to relax, twisting his soapy hands around and around, idly watch-ing a single droplet of the oily gel drip from the lip of the soap dispenser – plonk – into the water. He dried his hands at the same slow, measured pace, lost to the powerful furnace-like sound of the electric drier. It was there – off guard – his forehead pressed against the top of the drier and his whole head mildly vibrating that the thought of losing the Doyles first struck him as a real possibility. It was a choking sickly thought, one from which he was temporarily distracted by a memory of himself smiling at his own reflection in the big mirror in the Doyles' bathroom. That was a moment of unthreatened contentment, an assertion of just how happy he was to be there in that house among people who were always pleased to see him.

He rang Mrs Doyle to tell her about the delay. Two hours. No problem waiting. 'No problem, at all Mrs Doyle.'

She would get the message to Mr Doyle, figuring that Eugene would not be able to collect him much before one a.m.

The laden supper trolley was wheeled to the back of the room, away from the fire and covered loosely with a worn linen cloth kept specially for the purpose.

She had spent the greater part of her life preparing and serving meals. Ten maybe twelve people, her children and their friends, were regular numbers at the Doyles' table at supper time. And even though she now had only Mr Doyle to cook for, she approached each meal with the same sleeves-up gusto as she had in her heyday. She also continued to buy virtually the same quantities of food so the Doyles' fridge was always full. Rashers, eggs, pudding, liver, sausages, pounds and pounds of butter, cheese, chops, bowls of jelly, bags of sliced ham, eight, maybe ten, pints of milk and frying lard all packed so tight that it was impossible sometimes to see what was in the fridge. There was also an assortment of unusual products, vegetarian rissoles, meringue powder, soya steaks, items Mrs Doyle felt obliged to buy from some product promoter in the supermarket aisle.

Eugene stood underneath the flight information monitor for much longer than it should have taken to check there had been no further changes in the estimated arrival time of Eve's flight. When he was satisfied he headed back to the bar. He had been restored by Mrs Doyle's confidence, the warm, inclusive, almost conspiratorial tone of her voice, and he no longer battled with doubt or even recalled battling with doubt about his and Eve's future. He had about an hour and half to wait. Two slow pints.

The choice of dessert at the Good, Good and Stavely office party was between pavlova and *crème caramel*, but in practice everyone got both. Offering the choice was a routine the waitresses went through as they squeezed in between the tables, slapping both on to all plates in sight. Pavlova from the left, *crème caramel* from the right.

Mr Doyle had asked for *crème caramel*. A distant but familiar voice began to clamour. It was thin and feeble, the voice of a diminishing self, unable to break through the layers of self pity formed by the countless humiliations of the evening. He could no longer think of them in the order in which they had happened, so he just sat there, plum red and out of breath, defenceless against the next one; Hugh Thornley, in the distance on his way over from the directors' table to wish the pensioners Happy Christmas.

At first he thought it was the sombrero. Maybe people didn't know who was in there under that big straw umbrella of a hat. He took it off. He was still a has-been, a pensioner, part of a group of about twelve, herded and corralled into a corner every few minutes by Desiré Good. Doing his best to disguise his discomfort at having to rub shoulders with retired doormen and secretaries, Mr Doyle listened to Desiré Good instructing them to enjoy themselves.

'Let your hair down,' she urged. 'Do your own thing. We all want you to have a bally good night.' Her crinkly turtle eyebrow closed and reopened in what Mr Doyle refused to acknowledge as a wink in his direction.

'See you all back here in fifteen minutes. Photograph time.'

Mr Doyle's attempts to hide were only half-hearted. He knew Desiré Good well enough to know that trying to avoid her would be useless. She would search relentlessly until she had him back in that corner of the function room with the others, posing in his sombrero for the annual pensioners' photograph.

His attempt to appear happy was a form of protest. There was not a grain of happiness in his expression as he posed for the photograph, only an expression of enormous effort. The group, beginning to break up once the photograph had been taken, bunched back together again at the sound of a new command.

'We'll all meet in ten minutes over at the corner table, left hand corner,' she raised her left hand to point. Mr Doyle's lip curled as he watched the gilt chain of her evening bag slither over the parched skin of her fore-arm and lodge in the sinewy crease of her elbow.

'I have the seating plan in here.' She pointed at her sequinned evening bag, scrunching her face into its most scheming shape.

It came as no surprise to Mr Doyle to find himself on her right. 'I'm keeping Dick to myself,' she half-whispered, half-croaked, looking up coyly from the seating plan. The eyes of all the other pensioners were on him, waiting until he smiled at Desiré Good.

Four of five glasses of wine took some of the edge off waiting for Eugene. The message that Eve's flight had been delayed sent him hurtling back into panic. At that moment he was absolutely sure he could not stay there for another two hours. But the plan to leave – get a taxi home – was short-lived, because while he picked his way through the ifs and buts of changing the arrangements, contacting Eugene, having him paged at the airport, he spotted an unpoured bottle of wine at the far end of the table, a beckoning hand, promising no more thought.

The half finished plates of *crème caramel* and pavlova, littered with cigarette butts and discoloured by red dye running from soggy paper napkins, were whisked away. Coffee came and went as what Mr Doyle thought was a fire drill got underway. Some of the tables were folded and chairs were stacked on top of them. It occurred to him that the party might be over.

The moving of the furniture, the sound of a piano and drums and the dimming of the lights were not, from the swaying branch on which he was surveying it all, in any way connected, and so he was surprised when Desiré Good approached him with her armed crooked, ready to take the floor.

'So she wants to dance?' a cocky voice bellowed inside him as he scooped her up and swept across the floor to a thin but rhythmic version of 'In the Mood'.

It was on the cusp of one of those elaborate loop turns that Desiré Good, lost in the intimacy of the performance, whispered, 'You know I haven't said a word to a soul all these years.' As Mr Doyle looked blankly at her, she added, 'Not that it was ever any of my concern. Except of course as a Christian, to offer help. That's all I ever did, though I know you think differently.'

The dashing young Mr Doyle had vanished like a pick pocket, leaving Desiré Good in the hands of someone who had not heard or did not seem to have heard what she said, an exhausted Mr Doyle, who when 'In the Mood' finally ended, allowed himself to be guided to a seat.

'Thank you Dick.' Desiré spoke softly and with what sounded to Mr Doyle like exaggerated courtesy, as though she too had left a younger self out there on the dance floor.

She looked around the room, distracted, tapping the end of her unfiltered cigarette on her cigarette case. 'I'll leave you here to recoup but don't for a moment think you're going to escape with just one dance.'

Mr Doyle heaved himself out of his chair to go in search of his wine glass.

Chapter

7

EVE LISTENED intently, as Star described in a fanfare of tiny tinselly details the Christmas she had spent at her sister Pips's New Hampshire home two years previously. She animated each of Pips's family's Christmas rituals, moving her fingers, one moment like a puppeteer, the next like a harpist. And there were stories, whispered like secrets, as Star tip-toed down an imaginary stairs, opened a porch door and stretched her hand out to catch the snow flakes. Eve followed, picking her way through the crisp wafery snow, hearing Star and her nieces in the distance – laughing as they reached the crest of Maple Row Hill, all clutching the frayed rope of the old toboggan. It was a world of frosted windows billowing with the reflection of a roaring log fire, mornings spent curled up in the window seat, reading or just whiling away the hours before setting out, all muffled in scarves, on the river path to the frozen pond at Charterbridge. Eve listened, visualising every detail, mesmerised as a child watching the figures move in an elaborate clockwork theatre. As she went on listening small, unlikely details about Christmas at home began to surface and in their wake, a heady excitement. And if that excitement was shadowed by concern then she raced ahead and just snatched the joy it held, clutching it as though it had been stolen and was about to be reclaimed by some greater authority. In that way its downside, that vague sense of loss, the threat of having to abandon what she had become over the previous four months in Raleigh Reilly, remained unexplored and did not begin to unravel until she actually arrived home. Even then it unravelled in such a roundabout way that it was never more than partially in view, twisting and turning like a swirling kite tail.

Eve tried to guess who, among the tired, disorientated people gathered around the conveyor belt, owned the only incoming piece of luggage, a striped canvas suitcase. She fixed on a woman with turquoise winged glasses who watched it from the moment it first nosed through the flaps, but it sailed right past her. Eve's first thought, a thought which she instantly abandoned, was that the woman had made a mistake. A minute or two later the striped suitcase reappeared. This time everyone scrutinised it and, distracted by fatigue, Eve found herself wondering if it came through often enough would someone eventually claim it. She looked across at the people opposite. An elderly man in a checked shirt was straining forward to get a better view of it. When it was well out of reach and about to disappear through the exit hatch, he pointed at it. One or two people saw what was going on. The rest were unaware of a figure rushing from behind the old man and leaping on to the conveyor belt in an attempt to grab the suitcase for him. When he followed it through the exit hatch, those who did see him, including Eve, looked at each other for a reaction. Was it dangerous? Illegal? Funny? But before they could give each other any definite signals he came in the entry hatch, sitting cross-legged on the conveyor belt clutching the suitcase.

Someone in a group behind her said, 'easy known we're home'. Everyone laughed. It was as though something was being collectively rediscovered. Suddenly Eve stopped, tensing like a person struck by an unexpected memory. She did not want to participate in that collective rediscovery. She closed her mouth tightly and framed her face into the most serious expression she could manage. When her luggage came through, she snapped it off the belt and walked towards the arrivals hall, determined to remain firmly in possession of the person she had become in Raleigh Reilly.

When Eugene first glimpsed her he was overcome with relief. He bounced forward and immediately laid claim to her as if she were a lost child. He held both her arms, shook her, examined her, ran his hands up and down her arms, gripped her shoulders, looked at her intently and then finally – when he seemed to arrive at a point where he was absolutely sure it was her – enfolded her into an embrace that had a feel of permanence about it.

'We didn't know what was happening to you – where you were.'

Eve glanced around expecting to see her parents. She looked up at Eugene, waiting for him to point them out. All he saw in her questioning face was bewilderment which prompted the 'lost-child-found' response again. Only this time around it was all much faster. The gripping, shaking and examining were all part of one continuous movement ending in a tight clasp while Eve was still looking around for Mr and Mrs Doyle.

She and Eugene were well on the way before he managed to explain the arrangements. Eve asked for more and more details, trying to keep the conversation as impersonal as possible, but there was a limit to the number of questions she could ask and once it had been reached she knew the focus would change – which it did, sharply.

'Funny. Funny to think of the kind of things we got up to in that seat you're sitting in.'

'Why isn't Mam with him?' Eve paused, looking straight ahead into the darkness, aware that Eugene had glanced across at her a half dozen times since he said the first 'funny'. He drew breath, about to say something when she cut right across him, afraid he was going to continue along the same track.

'Why is he on his own? I mean it's not like him to be at the office party without her. She always goes.' As Eve spoke she tried to fend off a memory of sitting in the same seat, laughing when Eugene, leaning against her, twisting out of his clothes, drew back and activated the windscreen wipers with his elbow. Her upper lip curled as though she had tasted something sour. But when she stopped concentrating it gave way to a counter feeling which rapidly eroded the small space she had managed to forge between them, a space which almost disappeared altogether when it struck her how easy it would be to have sex with him again. The thought scampered around like an unruly child tugging her in the opposite direction to the one in which she wanted to go, mocking her resolve and firmly reuniting her with her past.

'You haven't changed a bit,' he said and by way of conclusion, although there was nothing to be concluded, he added 'not one single bit' – shaking his head and smiling into the darkness.

Eve wanted to say she had – to insist she had – but was afraid Eugene might take it as a challenge, something she was asking him to take into account in his plans for their future together.

'At what stage did you hear the flight had been delayed?'

'About ... just before it was due to arrive.'

'And you'd been there since you left Dad off. Where is it? Where's the party?'

'White's,' Eugene said, full of bounce, too preoccupied with how things were going to notice that he had already answered the same question in the arrivals hall and then later in the car park. Things were going well. He had attached too much importance to the fact that she had only written three times, all postcards, since September. Buoyed along by these consoling thoughts and happy just to have Eve beside him he turned towards her and in a voice charged with sincerity confided, 'You know I missed you a lot.'

This is the moment, Eve thought.

'It was great. Totally different to here, especially the way the courses work. And the way the lecturers are . . .' From there Eve went on to give such a precise description of her courses, her part-time job at Elbar, Star and all sorts of details about Raleigh Reilly that Eugene began to think he was, in some way unknown to himself, asking questions. He did not get a single opportunity to speak until they were on the way into White's Hotel.

When Eve saw her father in the sombrero, red-faced and breathless, second in the smaller of the two conga lines – a special pensioners' one organised by Desiré Good – she felt so overwhelmed by affection that she walked right out into the middle of the dance floor and threw her arms around him. And her joy took over completely, a fulsome uncomplicated feeling to which she abandoned herself all the more because it followed so closely on the chokingly tight half hour with Eugene. Desiré Good invited her to join in but Mr Doyle snapped such a sharp 'no' at her that she led the pensioners away and joined up with the main conga line which, to the sound of 'Viva Espagne', was weaving its way down the corridor towards the toilets.

Mr Doyle's welcome was no less warm until he remembered that Eugene should be there with them. He stood waiting, with one arm around Eve and the other suspended in the air, until Eugene took his place to make what Mr Doyle assumed was a happy trio.

The table at which her father was pointing seemed already full. He was speaking, explaining why they were going to that particular table, but Eve could not hear him above the bursting, brassy sound of the band. They were delayed for several minutes as the conga line, on its way back from the toilets, coiled around the crowded tables.

Earlier on Mr Doyle had discovered that one of the group at the table, Tadhg somebody-or-other, Eve didn't hear his second name knew Eugene. He was in full Indian regalia, complete with war paint and feathered head-dress. When he was introduced he sprang up dramatically and snatched her outstretched hand but immediately lost balance and slumped back onto his chair still holding Eve's hand. He then covered it with kisses and rapid as a cat lapping milk, began slipping his tongue in and out between her index- and fore-finger.

Nearby a young waitress was patiently taking last orders. A single string of her hair had become detached from the sleek main body. She looped it over her ear with her pen but it fell back straight away and hung loosely over the left side of her face. Mr Doyle was visibly agitated, unable to divert her attention from the Indians who kept increasing their orders from doubles to triples to quadruples. Eve sat down and although she was watching the peculiar movements of one of the Indians she was too preoccupied to work out precisely what he was doing. Only when she saw that he was being furtively goaded on by the Indian to his right did she begin to take definite notice. She watched as he lowered the half pint glass he had filled with Drambuie beneath the table and even leaned forward a little as he began to manoeuvre it, concentrating as if were tying his shoelace without looking. When he leaned back to let the Indian to his right see what he was doing Eve saw, but did not immediately believe, that he had put his penis in the drink.

'Here. Miss, this one is on us,' he said, full of hearty bon-homie, adding 'for yourself,' when the waitress tried to avoid taking the glass.

Mouthing a long protracted, 'No,' Eve jumped up and, com-bining a whole array of different warning signals – her hands, her eyes, her head – rushed towards the waitress.

'Don't worry I've no intention of touching it. I saw what he did.'

Eve looked at her, not convinced that she fully understood.

'Disgusting, but I've seen a lot worse,' the waitress announced flatly.

Eve stood looking at the two Indians, both bloated with laughter. Their eyes were tightly shut and their mouths wide open as they tried, in fits and starts, to tell the other Indians and Eugene what they had done.

The waitress finished taking the order, looped the stray string of hair over her ear with her pen and slapped her order-pad closed. As she passed Eve she stopped abruptly and, speaking through the side of her mouth like a cartoon undercover agent, whispered, 'At this stage I just double the bill.'

Eve smiled but was not consoled. Outwitting them was, in some ways, more distressing. It meant that they went unchallenged. It was, in principle at least, no different to the way her mother outwitted her father, always waiting for the right moment, the moment when she could redress the balance without being detected. It was a route which Eve decidedly did not wish to take, but at that moment in White's Hotel, the alternatives, which over the previous few months seemed so possible, were way out of reach.

Most of the way back to The Acre, Eve spoke about Raleigh Reilly, enthusiastically answering her father's questions, shooting off at tangents as she told him about this person and that, stopping to explain, to speculate and then racing along again. He smiled, a broad unchanging smile, hearing only her enthusiasm with its echoes of all her other enthusiasms down through the years. Only once, when she saw Eugene nod his head vigorously did her pace slow down. There was discomfort, a mild sense of betrayal in describing her life in Raleigh Reilly in such objective terms.

As they drove through the outskirts of the city, Mr Doyle began to make plans with Eugene about bringing the car back the following day. It was, they agreed, too late for Eugene to go in. Eve leaned back and as she looked out of the window at familiar landmarks shrouded in yellow street light, found herself thinking about her mother. When they arrived and found her napping in a chair beside the food trolley Eve was knocked off balance. The mother who had played such a prominent part in the endless theorising of the previous few months was nowhere to be seen. There was just Mrs Doyle, supreme in her world of crackling fires and food trolleys, a woman whose first few words were enough to exorcise that one-dimensional mother she was so often on the point of parading around the Equality Studies tutorial.

Eve looked around the room, mesmerised by how, in that first glance, everything appeared both familiar and novel at the same time. Mrs Doyle began to unveil the upper deck of the food trolley, telling herself that she should have put the butter in the fridge when she heard the flight had been delayed.

'But, no matter. All's well that ends well,' she said, leaving Eve speechless, a child whose parent stood between them and the world, endlessly making things right. Before she could say she wasn't hungry she found herself holding a plate with hard boiled egg sandwiches arranged like a bow-tie on a crisp white doily.

In the competition for Eve's attention Mr Doyle won hands down. He asked worldly questions, slowed her down if she tried to skip over some detail or other, whistled an oh-boy whistle to show how impressed he was, and, without giving it a thought, cut right across Mrs Doyle who readily gave way. Only when he whisked Eve upstairs to see her newly decorated bedroom, leaving Mrs Doyle holding the cup of tea she had poured for Eve, did she appear in any way put out.

'You have Eugene to thank for the wallpaper. His choice,' Mr Doyle said proudly.

Eve looked but said nothing. All her efforts went into making sure the 'Oh fuck' which was on the tip of her tongue stayed there. The wallpaper was lemony green with columns of tawny coloured guitars separated by bits of musical notation and song refrains like 'yeah, yeah, yeah'. These alternated with cameos of a couple dancing – the man clicking the fingers of his right hand and the girl twirling in a undulating dirndl skirt.

Her foreign doll collection which had been in the attic for years was on display again, sitting confidently on the curtain pelmet. There was a fluffiness about the place created by a range of boudoir accessories that Eve saw but did her best not to take on board. As she stretched her hand out to touch the new broderie anglaise dressing table cover, Mr Doyle spoke.

'I needn't tell you who chose that.' And drawing Eve into a conspiracy by arching his eyebrows and pursing his lips he nodded in the direction of the drawing room.

Eve felt suddenly protective of her mother, uneasy about entering into that conspiracy but at the same time helpless to do anything about it. She had become a spectator watching her own thoughts pass by, unwittingly disarmed by her parents' good intentions and generosity and rapidly re-entering life at The Acre as though she had never been away.

The question dominating conversations during the days leading up to Christmas centred on how many of his new family Noel should be allowed to bring to Christmas dinner. Mr Doyle said none but everyone knew that was a bargaining tactic, a position from which he could easily be persuaded to move. He wanted Noel, just as he wanted all his children there. If one of them was absent, his own position as head of the family would be incomplete, the collective strength of the group, his very lifeblood, diminished.

Mr Doyle's monitoring of Noel's progress had, from the beginning, been relatively relaxed. His decision to study sociology was his own as was his decision to drop out half way through the course to do what he called some 'real work' with the underprivileged. Mr Doyle did speak out at the time but it was not a relentless tirade as it might have been with Anton. After years of patient guidance by his wife, Mr Doyle had come to accept the notion of 'phases'. He did not believe, as she did, that all out-of-line behaviour was part of some phase or other. But he did see Noel's decision to drop out in that light and privately believed that he would eventually grow out of wanting to help the poor. Even if he didn't, Mr Doyle would probably have surprised everyone, particularly Anton and Syl, with his level of tolerance. Noel was not his failure, he was Mrs Doyle's. He believed that her involvement with meals-on-wheels had been a very bad influence on Noel. As a child Noel had spent far too much time at the centre. It was in that unreal atmosphere of hand-outs and cosy co-operation that his view of the world of work was skewed.

He would have preferred if Mrs Doyle had never had anything to do with meals-on-wheels. Initially he had agreed to her becoming involved because, after a hysterectomy following Eve's birth, she had spoken about her need for company with such uncharacteristic conviction that he became frightened. At one point during that brief but very difficult period it crossed his mind that she might even become unstable and lose her ability to cope altogether. On the advice of the family doctor who was also a good friend he encouraged her in her efforts to find an interest outside the home. When she fixed on meals-on-wheels and made an arrangement for Noel to come to the centre after school, Mr Doyle did not consider that the boy was in any way at risk. It was not until after Noel's decision to drop out, during one of the long protracted arguments which followed, that Mr Doyle first pointed out to Mrs Doyle that the decision was a direct outcome of her involvement with what he called 'that meals-on-wheels outfit'. She felt unfairly accused and asked him how on earth she could have been expected to see that it would all end so badly when it was something which even he himself had not envisaged at the time. But her defence, no matter how skilfully or unskilfully presented, did not save her from accepting the blame.

Noel wanted to bring three of his new family to Christmas dinner but was persuaded by Mrs Doyle to settle for two. She then suggested that he should bring them up for an hour or so some afternoon during Christmas week to let them get used to the place but Noel refused. They would not, he said in an accent which Mrs Doyle felt had deteriorated, 'take to the idea of a dry run'.

Noel had a way of putting things which Mrs Doyle sometimes found difficult to grasp. When he warned her about making him or any of his new family 'jump through the usual bourgeois Christmas hoops' she had to ask him what he meant and even then, after he had explained, she was still not sure if she had followed him correctly. She wondered why presents had to be ruled out.

'No presents on Christmas Day,' she repeated when he first said it charging her voice with surprise, hoping he had made a mistake.

'No,' he said emphatically. 'Buying presents supports the very system which has them where they are. It's an insult.'

Mrs Doyle wondered if this included giving them small tokens but did not ask, afraid he would say no. That, she thought, would be very awkward. Very awkward altogether, she almost said aloud, as she imagined the family sitting in the drawing room exchanging presents while Noel and the two men looked on.

'It would be hurtful,' she insisted, when Eve pointed out the reasons underlying Noel's stance on the presents. Not only did she find Eve's explanation unclear but she was irked by the way Eve had begun to sound more and more like Noel, talking accusingly about 'the system' as though Mrs Doyle was responsible for what happened in the world.

In his own way, Mr Doyle was reassuring. In a voice that sounded gruff but which she knew to be kind, he told her she was being foolish, getting into such a fuss about two no-hopers. Still, she remained apprehensive and right up until the moment they arrived was plagued by a sense of impending failure. She saw Christmas Day as a test of her efficiency and at a more profound level a reflection of her whole life's work.

She had invited Anton and Syl and their families for twelve, Noel and his new family for one. She hoped that by having them come an hour later they would simply be absorbed into the family rhythm. As it turned out, the hour was spent with Anton and Syl, much to Mrs Doyle's annoyance, joking about hygiene and contamination. Anton's wife Inez conspicuously volunteered to sit on one side of them and Eve on the other.

There was little or no agreement on what Noel's new family should be offered when they arrived. Mr Doyle said sherry on the grounds that Noel had asked that they be treated no differently than anyone else. Some of the others felt they ought to be given a choice. Stout was mentioned. Mr Doyle did have a dozen or so bottles on hand but when Mrs Doyle pointed out that the plain tumbler style glasses they would have to use would look very odd beside the ornate table glasses the idea was dropped.

When the doorbell rang everyone froze. Sabina, Anton's two-year-old daughter, frightened by the sudden silence, began to cry. Both parents rushed to her but Inez got there first and scooped her up, clutching her head and pressing it close to her own as though she were in great danger.

When Mr Doyle swept open the door, a man in his late middle age wearing an overcoat with a shoulder cape, walked straight past him and on into the drawing room, where, with the manners of an impresario he announced himself.

'George Dargell Defoe, late of Healy and Hume, fallen, you will no doubt note, on hard times.' He paused and with both his hands held up in a firm 'stop' pose, created the impression that the Doyles, all looking on incredulously, were plying him with questions.

'Yes, I'm afraid so,' he stage whispered. 'A small matter of embezzlement but,' and as he lingered on the word 'but', his voice soared up the scale, 'today, on the anniversary of the birth of Our Saviour,' he bowed his head reverently, 'I have been given an amnesty, a few brief hours of respite from a life soured by the deadliest of the seven deadly sins. Greed.'

He swung round dramatically on one heel to face Mrs Doyle directly.

'It is a very great pleasure, a very great pleasure indeed, to find oneself the recipient of such generosity.' He clasped Mrs Doyle's hands in his and bowed as he said, '*Enchanté, Madame.*'

More out of nervousness than amusement Syl's wife, Nuala, began to giggle. His head swung in her direction and with his thick bushy eyebrows rising and falling in quick succession, he told her she was the most beautiful woman he had ever seen. She covered her mouth with her hand and might have succeeded in smothering her giggle if he hadn't added that he was fortunate enough to have had occasion, at one stage in his life, to meet many beautiful women.

'Forfuxake,' Syl half whispered as he brushed past Anton, moving towards the drawing room door where his father, already out of patience with the second man, introduced by Noel as The Saint, was telling them to hurry up and make up their minds about what they wanted to drink. The Saint's eyes were downcast. He did not speak, then or at any point. Noel answered on his behalf, delaying for a few moments and looking directly at him as if by some secret process he was absorbing his responses.

'He'll have some lemonade,' Noel said confidentially but Mr Doyle was not listening. He was watching Mrs Doyle and George Dargell Defoe sweeping across to the drinks cabinet like a pair of professional ballroom dancers. And as they dallied in front of the open doors Mr Doyle was hard pressed to ignore the ease with which Mrs Doyle appeared to tolerate the flirtatious carry-on of Dargell Defoe. His ability to go on ignoring it was, within seconds, put to a test he could not hope to pass.

'Have we got any ... any Madeira?' Mrs Doyle asked in the faltering voice she sometimes used to ask him a question to which they both already knew the answer. It was her delicate way of asserting that as they had everything it was likely that they would have a bottle of Madeira in there somewhere. She expected that Mr Doyle, flattered by what she was implying, would be drawn into the charade.

'No, we don't.'

'Forgive me for asking,' Dargell Defoe pleaded, 'but it's a weakness of mine. I'm partial to a little Madeira at Christmas time.'

'There's plenty of sherry,' Mr Doyle said, affecting good humour but pleased that he wasn't making a good job of it.

Mrs Doyle put a fluted cut glass on top of the drinks cabinet and filled it with sherry for Dargell Defoe. Then, at his insistence, she took a second glass and poured one for herself. She turned and in a voice almost inaudible with politeness asked Eve if she would go into the kitchen and move the parsnips on to the slow plate and put the bread sauce up on the overhead rack. When she turned back she saw that Dargell Defoe had not only finished his own glass but hers too. She made a point of ignoring this just as she had made a point of ignoring his dirty fingernails and the black rim of his shirt collar. She refilled his glass, but not her own, and excused herself by pointing towards the kitchen and smiling apologetically.

Once inside she heaved a great sigh. Conspiratorial and good humoured, she was more at one with herself in those moments stolen from the world she herself had created than she was at any other time. Eve agreed when Mrs Doyle said she felt it was all running smoothly, but would not be drawn into any of the speculative chat which her mother tried to initiate.

'Is there something the matter?' Mrs Doyle asked.

Eve knew that there were any number of ways she might have said 'No' which would have encouraged Mrs Doyle to ask more questions so she was careful to say it in a light, offhand way, brushing the question aside as though she genuinely felt her mother was mistaken. At the same time, she began to think about how she would have liked to answer it.

'Is there something the matter?'

'I'm drowning, choking to death in this house.'

'Choking to death? Here? With your own flesh and blood, people who want nothing but the very best for you.'

'Yes. Choking to death' – and she was about to list the reasons why when Mrs Doyle's voice broke through.

'Remember Anton only likes a little stuffing, all white. Not a speck of brown and no stuffing at all for Daddy, but plenty of bread sauce.'

Inside in the drawing room George Dargell Defoe was going from one Doyle to the next and engaging their attention for as long as it took to pick up their glasses and scoff the contents. He had just reached Mr Doyle when news that dinner was on its way had everyone on their feet.

Mrs Doyle put a well heaped plate in front of him but he fell asleep before he had made any inroad into it. Conversation continued in whispers with Mrs Doyle tip-toeing back and forth to the kitchen, quiet as a mouse, delighted that it was all going so well.

Chapter

8

EVE WOKE, CERTAIN that there was someone in her room, someone she felt she knew. At first she did not open her eyes, afraid that whoever it was might be standing over her. After a few seconds in that tight-shut darkness she opened her eyes wide. Wide as wide can be. For an instant. Nothing.

She then began to wonder what it would be like to wake up after years and years in a coma, in unrecognisable surroundings among unfamiliar people. She pretended that the occasional sounds from the kitchen were sounds she had not heard before. And there were other sounds too, all undergoing some sort of transformation as she tried to imagine them as unrecognisable. In among them somewhere, straying around aimlessly, was a thought waiting to be grasped, a fact about the day to come from which, drifting in and out of sleep, she intuitively drew back. Almost in the same instant in which it occurred to her that it was New Year's Day she closed her eyes, pleased to remember that it was a day marked out for new beginnings. She speculated with little interest, lying there dozing off, full of the day and what it promised.

When she woke an hour or so later the impulse to avoid thinking about something was still there, stronger and more deeply rooted than it had been in her first waking. It was as though that impulse had remained awake like a vigilant watchdog, protecting her while she slept. The sensation that there was someone in her room returned, strutting like a jester, leading a parade of tumbling players and there in the centre of them, cart-wheeling along was the realisation that she and Eugene had, less than eight hours beforehand and without any reservations or discussion, had sex on the floor of the room she was in.

As she began to retrace her steps, vaguely hoping to discover that her part in the whole episode had been one of diminished responsibility, evidence to the contrary was rapidly piling up. The yacht club. New Year's Eve. All the Doyles. Left with Eugene. At ten, as arranged. Party. And there she came to a standstill, trying to recall the precise address. The car. They needed the car and had walked from the yacht club to The Acre to collect it. Three or four drinks by that stage. Three, she corrected herself, keen to be accurate once she had begun to gauge and at the same time minimalise the consequences of what had happened.

Her attempt to brush it aside, to regard it as a minor setback in the overall plan to be free of Eugene, might have been successful if it had not been based on the notion that there was no more to sex than the mechanics of a sexual encounter. As she mulled it over, reducing every movement, every point of engagement until it became detached from all the others, she remembered something Star had told her about a tribe of people she had been reading about who laughed in private but had sex publicly. Already she was planning to explain it to Star as a parting shot, something which had happened for old times sake. She imagined herself shrugging her shoulders, non-chalantly piecing it all together as she recounted how, in the end, she and Eugene had parted without either of them having to say it was over. She wondered if people ever really broke up like that, just walking away from one another, resigned to their fate like one of those couples in a French film. *Fin.* Lying there thinking about Star and the unpredictable course conversations with her could take, she began to wish she was back in Raleigh Reilly. And whenever another detail of sex with Eugene surfaced, triggering another bout of confusion, she discovered that she only had to tolerate it for as long as it took to remind herself that within twenty four hours she would be on her way back.

When she was organising her flights in mid November, she had considered a later return date, but the Elbar P. S. Division, always particularly busy during school vacations, had eleven operations ready to run that week, over a thousand dollars' worth of work. She couldn't afford to turn it down. And besides, Star was due back from New Hampshire on the same day which was a big bonus.

In the kitchen her mother was racing around opening the oven door, closing the oven door. Turning on taps, turning off taps. Opening the fridge, the cupboard, moving chairs – eternal sounds, the countdown to yet another meal. And Eugene was an integral part of it all, tightly woven into the tapestry. Eve wished there was something overwhelmingly wrong with it, some great injustice at its core, something she could easily walk away from. But there wasn't. There was only the predictability, days and days and days, all indistinguishable from each other.

The kitchen in Eugene's home, the only place in the tall sparsely furnished terraced house in which he and his mother ever met, had none of the clamour and bustle of the Doyles'. Every surface was damp with condensation. The window looking out on the featureless back yard – one dustbin and a pale yellow saucer for a ginger cat that came and went – was awash with thin wobbly threads of water that gathered pace as they flowed down and then splashed on to the mildewed sill. Sitting on top of the low black range, which was never lit, was a small white enamel two-ringed electric cooker. High above,

91

strung up and held in place with pulleys and ropes was a long wooden airer. It was there, underneath a canopy of damp clothes that Mrs Wall had spent the greater part of her life.

That morning like every other morning she stood beside the table. She did not know when Eugene would come down. It could be as late as noon but that didn't trouble her. Her ability to wait was second to none. She could stand beside the flecked Formica-topped table for hours, still as a palace guard. Ironically, when Eugene appeared she never stayed in the room for more than a few minutes, just long enough to serve his breakfast. If she returned then it was only to refill his teacup and ask him if there was anything else he wanted. It was such a familiar routine that he would have been hard pushed to imagine any other.

When he pounded down the stairs the whole house jerked into life, bracing itself for his brief stay like a sleepy railway station tensing to the arrival of a train. Mrs Wall had long since given up asking him even the most uninvasive of questions. She had not noticed that he was beginning to emerge from the long years of silence and might have disclosed more about his world if she had enquired. So she was surprised that morning when, before he even started to eat his breakfast, he asked her if the shops were open on New Year's Day. She had learned to make the most of any snippets of conversation which trickled her way and spun out her answers as though they were about to have a full scale conversation.

'It depends.'

He didn't reply.

'Some are and some aren't. It depends on the kind of shop.'

'Jewellers'.'

'No, but I wouldn't be sure.'

She refilled his teacup and waited while he scooped out the top of his egg, handing her the empty shell as he turned the spoon in his mouth and drew it out slowly through his tightly closed lips. She hovered about for a few minutes, peering into the sugar bowl, the milk jug, the butter dish to see if they could be topped up. All were brimful so she left and hurried upstairs clutching the word 'jewellers'' as though it were an object she urgently wanted to examine.

In her bedroom she took full stock of the word but only for a spilt second because it filled her with such fear that she knelt down by her bedside and started to pray. These were desperate pleading prayers, some of which she abandoned after the first few words, launching recklessly into others which, in her turmoil, she hoped would provide more relief. Terrified that the thoughts from which she was running were catching up, she looked over her shoulder and there they were, led by Jeweller, galloping towards her like a Western posse. Engagement Ring. Marriage. The end of the world as she knew it.

When she heard the front door closing she stood up and tiptoed across to the window. Through a narrow gap where the heavy appliqué curtains joined she watched Eugene unlocking Mrs Doyle's Mini and climbing into the driver's seat. She stood stoically, resigned to her lot, like the captain of a sinking ship watching the last lifeboat disappear into the distance.

In the lazy hours following a family lunch at The Acre the Doyles' drawing room sometimes took on the appearance of an ante-room in a casualty clinic. The way they sat, slumped and splayed, gave the impression that they had been in some mysterious way struck down. Sprawling limbs – and in particular on that New Year's Day Eugene's legs, one of which was flung over the arm of the chair and the other parked straight out in front of him – made the chairs and couch, large as they were, seem inadequate.

As soon as Inez left with Sabina to visit her own parents, Anton fell asleep. His head fell back over the curved top of his armchair and his Adam's apple, chin and nose rose like three sharp peaks pointing towards the ceiling. Syl, twitching in and out of sleep, lay partly blanketed by the fanned pages of a newspaper. The only one not afflicted by that mid-afternoon malaise was Mrs Doyle. Like a ministering angel she went from chair to chair offering chocolates from a box so large that every step she took had to be considered. As she cautiously manoeuvred her way around the room she leaned slightly forward, straining as she did when she brought the large tea-tray in every night after the ten o'clock news. If one of them dallied, as Mr Doyle did, she assisted, listing the wide selection: 'Nougat, Turkish Delight, Caramel, Hazelnut.' He looked up at her as she spoke, smiling through a haze of port and asked her to choose for him.

'Turkish Delight,' she said formally, smarting like a young nurse playfully fending off a flirtatious elderly patient. She rested the corner of the box on the coffee table and picked out a barrel shaped chocolate, holding it up between her forefinger and her thumb until he nodded. She cast her eyes downwards when, instead of his hand, he briefly offered his open mouth. Then full of the playful self-righteousness he enjoyed so much she handed it to him in a business-like way.

Endless, frequently repeated moments like this had piled up over the decades, forming layers in the way that shells and bones calcify over millennia into rock. They formed an imperceptible bulwark against the world, endlessly rebuffing all that came its way. Both knew that far away across the estuary was another world. But at times like that, lazing in the drawing room after a long meandering lunch, that world was a speck in the firmament.

In making it all run so smoothly Mrs Doyle led the way, interpreting Eve's unwillingness to follow was a failure on her own part, one she hoped she could undo by good example. That was partly the spirit in which she offered the chocolates, listing the choices and telling them all how much they were going to enjoy the one they had selected.

Eve, who was sitting in a lotus position beside Nuala on the couch stretched out to take a chocolate but changed her mind saying, 'No, maybe I won't,' while her hand still hovered over the box.

Nougat? Turkish Delight? Caramel? Hazelnut? Mrs Doyle felt Eve needed encouragement, time to think, and so stood in front of her waiting, sure she would change her mind and dip in. When she didn't and a moment later Eugene didn't either, Mrs Doyle saw their refusals as yet another mark against herself. And although there were scarcely any grounds for doing so, she added that episode, if it could be called an episode, to a number of others which since Eve came home re-enforced her sense of inadequacy. She wondered how she could make amends, what she could do to liven things up for Eve and Eugene.

'Anyone for a game of twenty-fives?' she asked, rearranging the ornaments on the crowded sideboard with her elbow, hoping against the odds to clear enough space for the chocolate box.

'Me. Count me in. I'll play, Mrs Doyle,' Eugene piped up. Eve drew breath evenly, about to answer, when they heard a light, single knock on the front door.

Mrs Doyle turned around, looking for confirmation mainly from Eve and Nuala that it was a knock and at the same time implying, with her taut lips and crinkly forehead, that she considered it a peculiar time for a visitor. Mr Doyle sat up, recognising the all-hands-on-deck routine the Doyles went into whenever there was a knock at the front door. Syl raised his head and shook it, loosening his jaws and wobbling his cheeks. He then sat forward and shook his whole body like a dog after a swim, forcing himself into a full waking state. Anton didn't move.

Mrs Doyle had not managed to clear enough space on the sideboard for the chocolates and stood holding the box. She nodded in the direction of the front door, indicating that Eve should answer it. With the same thinly disguised reluctance to co-operate which marked many of her dealings with her family that Christmas, Eve disentangled herself from her lotus position and headed for the door. She stayed out in the hall for several minutes talking, leading those inside who were curious, Eugene and Mrs Doyle, to assume that one of her friends had called. Then her head appeared in the doorway. Very briefly.

'I'm going out.'

She just flung the words among them. Mrs Doyle looked at Eugene, pleading with him in an affectionate sort of way to be patient with Eve, implying with her soft smile that he should not follow her, which he was just about to do. He was quick on the uptake. They had become confidantes, he and Mrs Doyle, discussing Eve whenever they were alone. Initially it had begun in a very circumspect way with Mrs Doyle gingerly edging forward behind reliable old shields – 'It's none of my business, but ...' – expecting to retreat at any moment. But Eugene had been so forthcoming, so quick to disclose how confused he was by Eve, that Mrs Doyle found herself reassuring him and even occasionally apologising on Eve's behalf.

A minute or so after Eve's first appearance in the doorway she was back again. She seemed to be trying to decide whether to come in or not. She fixed on Mr Doyle in such a deliberate way that he looked about the room, wondering if there was something wrong. When he found everything as it should be he relaxed, taking out his handkerchief and working his way slowly through the ritual of blowing his nose.

Eve drew back and closed the door noiselessly, releasing the handle as though she had been spying and had heard or seen something of significance.

When she returned an hour later she walked, almost stomped, into the room, leaving nobody in any doubt, except Anton, that she was there with a mission. Behind her stood a girl of her own age, someone Eugene was so certain he recognised that he pointed, confident that her name was just about to roll off the tip of his tongue. He was still pointing, still hoping to hear himself say her name when Mr Doyle, in a way with which they were very familiar, shouted, 'News, quick turn on the television.'

The six-thirty 'News' was an event of major importance in the Doyle household. The word itself, NEWS, belonged more with emergency cries like FIRE or HELP than it did with words announcing a routine household event. Everything came to a standstill as the greater world beyond The Acre, the world in which Mr Doyle had a firm foothold, took precedence. In the kitchen at eight in the morning, the sitting room at six-thirty and ten, whoever was around might find themselves being aggressively hushed into silence by Mr Doyle. It was a response so ingrained that the signature tunes were in themselves enough to bring about a sort of temporary paralysis. Since Mr Doyle retired he had an even greater need to assert his loyalty to the world beyond. Consequently he now not only listened to the usual news broadcasts but took in all the hourly summaries as well, sometimes turning up the volume dramatically, cutting Mrs Doyle off in mid-sentence. She didn't mind. What she did mind, and minded a great deal more than Mr Doyle knew, was the way he expected her to turn off the washing machine or the vacuum cleaner. This slowed down her progress making her resentful about 'The News' in a way she never had been before he retired.

None of the Doyles knew what to do when Eve stood in front of the television, entirely blocking their view of it. It was an act of outright sabotage, carried out before the broadcaster had finished reading the first item.

They waited, certain that Mr Doyle would sound a war cry which would have them all back viewing within seconds. But he didn't. He was bewildered, hopelessly casting around for an explanation.

'Look. Take a good look. Today's "News" is here.' Eve pointed to the back of the room where the girl who had come in with her stood apologetically.

Nuala put down her cards, face upwards as though she knew

at that point she would not be resuming the game of twenty-fives she had been playing with Eugene and Mrs Doyle.

'Well? Doesn't anyone want to know who she is?'

'Who is she? introduce her,' Mrs Doyle urged, ready as always, to smooth the ruffles. Eve looked at the girl, at first expectantly and then reassuringly.

'It's taken her a hell of a lot of courage to walk into this house,' Eve said solemnly, unnerving her mother by the twangy way she inflected the end of the sentence.

Mrs Doyle smiled, a fulsome smile held for so long that it changed to an expression of acute pain.

'I'm sorry for coming. Like this, here.' She pointed to the surroundings, holding her hand in mid-air, spreading her fingers and then bunching them together, as she went over to Eve. 'I've come as far as the gate before. I knew if I didn't come in this time ... So I made it a New Year's resolution.' Her lips moved as though she were about to continue speaking but nothing followed.

To the Doyles' amazement, Eve put her arm around the girl's shoulder. She began to cry, shaking in an effort not to, bowing her head and curling in on herself.

'I'm not usually like this,' she said between sobs.

The tightly clenched atmosphere might have loosened a bit if Mr Doyle had said something when through her tears the girl smiled apologetically at him. But he only sank further into his chair, visibly diminishing, cowering in a way that made everyone look away. Syl was first to come to his defence.

'What's going on here?' His voice sounded so like his father's that for a brief moment Mrs Doyle felt things were returning to normal.

Eve began to answer Syl's question in a carefully measured way. 'She came here ...' when the girl suddenly cut in, 'No. I'll say what it is.' But then she paused.

Mrs Doyle appeared to be listening as attentively as the others. She even had the same expectant expression, looking directly at the girl. But she was only partly aware that the girl, in fits and starts, was struggling to say something. Mrs Doyle was too pre-occupied, too concerned with how put out she felt the others, particularly Mr Doyle and Eugene, were by the intrusion. Eve, she believed, was pushing Eugene's tolerance to the limit, standing there in front of the television telling everyone what to do. If it had been an isolated incident, then maybe ... but her speculation ended as the long list of the ways Eve had tried Eugene's patience that Christmas unrolled. Unable to bear thinking about the consequences, she turned her attention to Mr Doyle. She began repeating bits of 'The News' to herself, planning haphazardly to present them to him when he erupted. This, she was absolutely certain, he was about to do at any second. She latched on to an East European name, Polnsky, and tried to piece together an understanding of the event or what seemed like the series of events in which he was involved. She knew as she said that name over and over again just how inadequate a peace offering it would be, but still she continued, afraid, if she stopped, of hearing what the girl was saying.

When Eva noticed that her mother had turned towards the television and was straining to follow 'The News', she turned it off. Within a few seconds the girl paused again before saying, 'so that's about it'. She looked at Mrs Doyle who smiled – warm and reassuring as always.

In the glacial silence which followed, Eve surveyed her family, one by one, in search of allies. The survey stopped when she got to Mr Doyle but the showdown she was working her way towards and which she tried to bring to a head by saying, and then virtually shouting, 'Well,' never happened. He sat slumped, his eyes downcast, calm but in a deeply dejected way, already swaddled in self pity, fully insulated against any challenge she or anyone else might aim in his direction.

Syl stood up and stretched slowly. He extended his arms

and unfurled his clenched fists by flicking each of his fingers individually from the palm of his hand. His low straining stretch-growl turned to speech without losing any of its gravelly tone. 'It's time we were off.'

Before he spoke Nuala's head began to wag mechanically, eagerly agreeing to what she was absolutely certain he was about to say. With that they backed towards the door, taking it in turns to say, 'Thanks for everything.'

Anton stirred when the door closed and for a brief moment it seemed as though he was about to wake up. As he began to drift off again Eugene sighed, a single effort-filled balloon-blow of a sigh, gauged to place himself in the same straits as the others whom he believed were longing for any sort of distraction.

'Now, what we all need is a cup of hot tea.' Mrs Doyle leapt up and, oblivious to the sea of disbelief around her, went in her usual pit-pat way to the kitchen. Eve watched her leave the room and then as though Mrs Doyle had left behind something of great importance, dashed after her. As she passed she grasped the girl's wrist and with a series of quick head flicks indicated that she would be back shortly.

Mrs Doyle was skidding around the kitchen, tea-tray – over beside the fridge, teacups – in the cabinet, tea caddie – on the shelf over the cooker, tea cosy – in the dish cloth drawer, teapot – on the back of the cooker, teaspoons – in the cutlery drawer. Eve stood at the door, not at all sure she was going to be able to break into the fortress of tea-making in which her mother had so successfully taken refuge. Mrs Doyle was first to speak.

'Polnsky. Or is it Polmsky? I can't for the life of me get the hang of those names.'

Her words followed her around the kitchen as she flapped like a trapped bird landing on the fridge, the kitchen cabinet, the shelf over the cooker.

'Can't you see how hard it was for her to come here?' Even

as she spoke Eve knew there was an audible undercurrent of anger in her question.

'Well, a good cup of hot tea ... she'll be all the better after a good hot cup of tea. We all will.' Mrs Doyle disappeared into the clouds of steam as she poured the boiling water into the teapot. When she reappeared she was smiling. 'Now you hold the door open,' she half-whispered, 'and before you know it we'll all have a nice cup of hot tea in our hands.'

There were bank statements, dozens of them strewn among the upturned cards on the coffee table. Mrs Doyle nodded to Eugene, smiling. 'If you wouldn't mind.' He began to clear the table, quickly scooping up the cards and the papers so Mrs Doyle could put down the large tea-tray. The girl stretched out to take the bank statements. She wanted above all else to impress on the Doyles that she felt no acrimony.

'Sugar?'

'Yes please.'

'One or two.'

'One please,' the girl said, bundling the bank statements back into the shoulder bag from which she had produced them five minutes earlier.

'Now that Nuala is gone,' Mrs Doyle said wistfully, 'would anyone else ...' She tilted her head in the direction of the cards which Eugene was lazily shuffling. 'Maybe you ...' and she smiled fulsomely at the girl.

'Yes. I mean no. No. Thanks all the same.' And speaking directly to Mr Doyle, she said, 'I'm sorry for coming.' He raised his head a little giving everyone the impression that he was about to speak to her. When he didn't, Mrs Doyle came to the rescue.

'Daddy is exhausted,' she announced, repeating the word and pitching it into the void which had swallowed up, without trace, her first attempt to deflate the sense of expectancy he had created by moving his head. The girl sidled over towards the door, followed – and at the same time led – by Mrs Doyle.

'Goodness me. That's a very light jacket for a night like this. Let me see if I can find you something warmer.' Mrs Doyle turned to leave the room before the girl had a chance to explain that her coat was hanging in the hall. In that moment Eve bounced up and stood between the girl and the door.

'You can't go.' She shook her head adamantly. 'You're not going like this.'

Eugene, who had slid in beside Eve, put his arm around her shoulder. He began to whisper into her ear when she swung around and confronted him directly.

'If you have something to say then say it out loud. And take your arm away.'

'Come on Eve. This isn't an easy situation for any of us.' He went on to say something about sticking together but it got lost in the whirl-wind as Mrs Doyle entered, holding her old musquash fur by the shoulders, ready to put it on the girl.

'Take that back,' Eve commanded, stopping Mrs Doyle in her tracks, but immediately regretting the force with which she had spoken. As Mrs Doyle skidded to a halt, Eve had caught a glimpse of the hysteria underlying her mother's relentless goodwill.

'I'm coming with you.' Eve made it clear that she had already made up her mind and did not need the girl's agreement. Eugene was unsure of what he ought to do. He stood, towering above the group, looking down at Mrs Doyle for guidance. But she herself was stranded on the sideline clearly anxious to intervene but unable to get a foothold.

'Count me in, too.' He beamed at Eve. 'May's well. At this stage I think we'll all agree that a pint wouldn't go amiss. All right if I take the car, Mrs Doyle?' Eugene tried to sound as normal as possible and to his own mind was succeeding admirably. In an attempt to wrap it all up he clasped his hands together and added, 'I'm sure you won't say no to a lift.'

Mrs Doyle was too intimidated by the intensity with which Eve was looking at her to respond to Eugene's request.

'I think I'm ruffling a few feathers here,' he smirked, 'but nothing a drink or two won't settle.' He licked his lips and rolled them together, letting his eyebrows rise and fall, completing his most self-satisfied, job-well-done expression.

'I'd prefer if you didn't come,' Eve said coldly, prompting Eugene to laugh.

'Easily known when you're not wanted.' He laughed louder, at the same time searching Eve's expression to gauge how serious she was.

'OK. I'll give you a head start. A half an hour. I'll be in Lahey's in half an hour,' and like a referee nearing the end of a match, he conspicuously checked his watch, 'half seven. On the dot.'

Mrs Doyle put down the mottled fur coat and attempted to take charge. She raised both hands simultaneously and held them in front of her like she did when she was preparing to roll wool. She was all set to make an announcement and clearly pleased with what she was going to say but delayed to savour the encouragement Eugene was beaming down on her. His attention remained fixed on her while Eve began to speak.

'Look Eugene. We are not going to Lahey's,' and then full of the sort of self possession which Eugene had come to dread more and more that Christmas, 'surely you get the point. I don't want you to come with us. In fact I don't want you. Full stop.'

Eve saw but did not register Eugene's response. Her determination to suppress the voice demanding that she turn what she had said into a joke, required all the concentration she could muster.

Mrs Doyle shivered. She braced herself to speak again but was, for the second time, left standing, powerless to stop Eve.

And just in case you think it was a spur of the moment remark, I'll repeat it . . .' Suddenly she was in full flight, unexpectedly on course. And she would have continued if Mrs Doyle had not rushed at her and with more force than anyone would have thought she possessed, pushed her. She tumbled back, unsure of what was happening. The thin smile, barely rippling Eve's lips, was one of bewilderment. As she straightened up she saw her mother grabbing her old fur coat from the chair and clasping it as she might a recently bereaved friend. When Mrs Doyle spoke her voice was calm and almost unrecognisable without its hissy warmth.

'Yvonne, you go along with . . .'

'Mary,' the girl said.

'That's the right thing to do now,' Mrs Doyle added, stealing a glance in Mr Doyle's direction. But he had sunk so far into his sagging armchair that only his legs – from the knees down – could be seen.

With every step Mrs Doyle took, Eugene took a step in the same direction. Gradually they made their way back to the hearth. When Eve opened the front door the through-draught caused the drawing-room door to bang closed and Anton woke with a start, cold and disorientated.

'God. Things are very quiet around here. What's going on?'

'Nothing. We're going to have a game of twenty-fives. You'll play. Won't you? Inez and Sabina won't be back for another half an hour. There's tea in the pot. Let me get you a cup.'

Still uncoiling from sleep, Anton didn't know what he wanted, so by default he drifted into playing twenty-fives and drinking tea.

Eve did not know what to expect when, around midnight, through sheets of thin flinty rain, she arrived back at The Acre. She felt weighed down physically, limb-weary, with all that she had heard. She was trying to recall, as she had many times that evening already, an afternoon which Mary had spoken of, when they had played together on a beach. Mary had showed her a photograph taken by her mother. There they were, two spindly girls, Mary about six and Eve seven, smiling, their heads leaning to one side, each with one arm crooked over her forehead squinting into the sun. Eve had kept picking it up and examining it, trying to grasp the fact that without knowing it, she had for a very long time been a significant part of someone else's life. Mary's unquestioning acceptance of that and her mother's other secret schemes to bring her into contact with the Doyles made it all the more difficult for Eve to take on board. The matter-of-fact way Mary spoke about her life left Eve with the sensation of belonging to an impoverished narrative, a story that was becoming more incomplete by the minute.

As her story surged ahead of itself, it left half familiar names, uprooted signposts, in its wake. Like Desiré Good who, when Mary's mother Bernadette, a secretary at Good, Good and Stavely, discovered she was expecting a baby, had enthusiastically taken over all the arrangements. Down through the years she had been an occasional visitor to their home in Calvery Terrace and over the previous eighteen months had been encouraging Mary to approach her father and step-brothers and sister.

Eve shuffled through the dark hall, relieved that there was nobody about. Every now and then she came to a standstill, marooned by the sensation that the space through which she was edging her way forward was unfamiliar. Each time that sensation recurred, it linked up with the previous time, cumulatively draining her of the confidence to move forward without the fear that she was about to crash into something. She stood in the grip of that fear, trying to impress upon herself that she was standing in the doorway of the dining room in her own house when, clear as a bell, her mother's voice sounded from inside.

'I don't want this sorry business mentioned again.'

Eve did not go in but edged the door a little more open, enough to see Mrs Doyle, wearing the old musquash, sitting like Banquo's ghost at the table which was still strewn with the lunchtime debris, including the clean-picked, dried-out carcass of the goose.

In that one glimpse Eve saw that Mrs Doyle had got the whole picture. With that she lost sight of all she had to say about the reception Mary had been given by the Doyles. When she approached her mother, hoping to discuss what had happened, Mrs Doyle sprang up from her chair.

'You have such an early start and Daddy was so tired that I decided to ring for a taxi to take you to the airport in the morning.' She smiled, a fulsome smile. 'I'll say my goodbyes now, 'and she stretched her arms out to embrace Eve. The smell of mothballs from the old fur mixed with all that powdery warmth and fading perfume sent Eve racing back to a time when there had been nothing outside the world of that tight grasp. The fact that there was now – and so much to boot – prompted a sort of muted sobbing which Mrs Doyle seemed to absorb without actually acknowledging.

From her bedroom Eve heard Mrs Doyle rummaging about. Well used to the late night shut-down sounds, she paid little attention. But the noise level began to increase, working its way up to a busy hum, broken by the clatter of crockery and the chugging jolt the pipes made when the water was turned on. By one a.m. the whole house reverberated with loud clanging noises, saucepans thrown into cupboards, pans slapped on to the range, cutlery flung into the drawer – all underscored with mop slaps and the whack of the floor brush against the skirting board. Mrs Doyle was washing up and cleaning with a vengeance, reclaiming territory that had been under siege. And she was making headway, solid empowering progress, every surface and every crevice, systematically destroying the forces which threatened the harmony of life at The Acre.

Chapter

9

EVERY EVENING, DURING that first raw, icy week back on campus Eve expected to find Star slumped in the bean bag, back from New Hampshire with a big tangle of stories about Christmas. When she had not arrived by Friday, Eve gave up any hope of seeing her before the following Tuesday, when the semester officially began. Again and again she went over the arrangement they had made. Their plan to return on the same day had been worked out weeks ahead of the Christmas vacation when Eve was trying to make up her mind about taking on extra work at Elbar. Star had been very persuasive, rattling off all the advantages of being back on campus before everyone else arrived. When Eve tried to think of what these advantages were all she could remember was the way Star kept saying 'and as well as that'. And as well as that, what? she said to herself, trying to coax the forgotten advantages to the surface.

It began to snow early on the Friday evening as Eve walked towards the great columned entrance of the Behavioural Sciences block on her way to ring Mary Byrne from the call box outside the ground floor cafeteria. The large double doors to the lobby were open but there was no access to any other part of the building. She stood on the steps, going through the places on campus where other pay phones were located.

Someone passed by, cowering as though the light flecky, snow was a full-scale storm. In a uninterested sort of way she watched the figure disappear into the snow. Without a whit of notice to herself, Eve burst into tears. She did not have answers to the fleeting shoals of questions which, every so often, coursed through her mind. In the space they left behind were loose unanchored feelings, all different sides of a loneliness which she was unwilling to name.

It was a help to fix on the abduction which had gone seriously wrong the previous afternoon. Posing as the Nebraskan aunt and uncle eight-year-old Evan Fisher had never met, Eve and Rube North, an experienced Elbar employee, stopped, as planned, to pick Evan up at his school friend, Marty Faldon's house. They told him that they had arrived ahead of time for their overnight visit and as a treat had been allowed to collect him. It was a double take, involving Marty Faldon's parents who, as soon as Evan was in the car with Rube and Eve, headed with Marty straight for Elbar to take part in the post abduction therapy session. Once Evan had opened the gifts they had brought he calmly told them that they were not his uncle and aunt from Nebraska.

'But of course we are. What a crazy thing to say.' Rube always took the lead.

Evan did not reply but at the next set of traffic lights tried to get out of the car which was, by the strictest of Elbar regulations, child-locked. From then on in it was a full scale battle with Evan screaming and pounding, pulling Rube's hair and gesturing wildly at passing motorists. When they finally got to the dispatch point, a supermarket parking lot, they had to drive around and around the crowded parking blocks for almost fifteen minutes, pleading with him to calm down as they tried to locate his parents' black Buick. He saw it first and dived over Rube's shoulder, grabbing the steering wheel. When he failed to turn it he sank his teeth into Rube's shoulder. As soon as the car stopped, Eve opened her door and pressed herself back against the seat making way for him to climb across. He was over and out before either of them had time to make the on-site regulation contact with his parents.

Eve's reservations about the P. S. I love you programme, never at any stage very far from the surface, got what at the time seemed like a sympathetic hearing from Rube. He told her that every doctor and dentist in the United States had stories to tell about a kid whose resistance to preventative treatment, inoculation or whatever, was way out of line. It was a part of the job, he said and then, after a long bout of concentration, 'Sometimes you gotta be cruel to be kind.'

When Eve arrived at work the following day, Larry, smiling in his usual welcoming way, told her he had taken her off the operation lined up for that morning so they could talk, 'You know, about how things are going generally.' Rube, he explained, had filed a report on the Fisher–Faldon operation and he felt he would like to hear her version of events. She started by giving a concise account, fixing on the gaps in the profile supplied by the Fisher family. But as more and more details of Rube's report filtered into Larry's questions Eve began to see that she was, in fact, being interrogated. When it emerged that Rube had at one point in his report described her as 'passive' she had difficulty remaining coherent and lapsed into 'Yeahs' and 'Fines' and 'OKs'. But even in those brief replies there was a wobble which prompted Larry to reassure her.

'It was an unusually difficult case.'

Eve was partly consoled, more by the avuncular tone than anything else. The word 'passive' stayed with her all morning, yelping and tripping her up. She wished that Star had come back, and began to imagine what she might say about Rube. About Larry, about everything. But imagining wasn't enough and as always her family and Mary were there, impatiently bobbing up and down in the background, waiting for the slightest lull to rush in and stake out a position in the forefront of her thoughts.

When she rang home two days previously Mrs Doyle had sounded the same as always, delighted to get the call, full of news, talking at break-neck speed, filling every crevice in the conversation with the minutiae of life at The Acre and its satellites, Au beau Ciel, Anton's house, and Dun Roamin, Syl's house. Eve listened carefully, aware that between the lines and only between the lines would she get a view of how things stood. And there was the constant risk that Mrs Doyle would begin to panic about the cost of the call and hang up at a few seconds' notice.

Still, by meticulously picking her way over the conversation afterwards, Eve was able to isolate the previously invisible microbes of information which most interested her and fuse them together to produce an approximate picture of the state-of-play at The Acre. In that way she surmised that her parents were taking every possible step to avoid being in each other's company but that when they did cross paths things were as they always had been, with Mrs Doyle working to make sure it all ran smoothly. There were, however, some indications that they were becoming more skilled at avoiding each other. Mrs Doyle had discovered that her sister Mona, 'a bit low after Christmas' had sunk into a 'worrying depression' and 'out of common decency' she felt that the least she could do was keep her company during the day. The only drawback was the discomfort she felt in knowing that Mr Doyle didn't relish the cold meat salads she left for him.

'Not that he has said anything. I've hardly seen him. He's gone by the time I get in, the yacht club one evening, the golf club the next.'

Eve knew that contacting them was not the answer to the sense of panic she felt. She would only hear more of the same, good cheer that was thrown like a fire blanket over everything that went on at The Acre. At the same time she continued to believe that they were all moving to a point where everything –

and she had an increasingly long list of injustices – would be acknowledged.

Eve saw Mary Byrne as a fixture in their lives. Sometimes she imagined that she had known about her all along, not in a conscious sense but as a presence she could not define. Her arrival on New Year's Day had momentarily revealed a graphic view of something Eve knew was part of her own story. She wanted to put words to it, to understand it but the forces which had always kept things in their place in the Doyles' world had moved in like white corpuscles to the site of an infection, isolating it and leaving the rest, the full recovery of the system, to time. Those forces, though pushed to their limits, had somehow managed to win the day. Even though she did not know how to go about it, Eve was determined that the victory would not be permanent.

She stepped out on to the snow, picking her way forward as though she were walking on a surface that could at any moment crack and break open. Distracted by the flossy crunch of her footsteps she began to fantasise about coping with some overwhelming family problem, violence, chronic alcoholism, the sort of difficulties which had brought people in the Equality Studies literature to a precipice, to a point where they got the whole picture, and were left with no choice but to turn around and forge a future for themselves. In that way there would be little or no lingering guilt, no sense of disloyalty. She slowed down, looking at the ground as though she had spotted something in the melting snow, lumbered by the thought that her family regarded any step she took out of the general orbit of their world almost as a betrayal. That thought might have focused her thinking if it had not been immediately followed by the idea of calling on Irma Knoll to ask if she could use her phone. Just a short call, she said to herself, already planning to explain why she needed to ring.

Irma Knoll lived at the edge of the lower playing fields, just outside the campus. Her apartment consisted of one large room partitioned into alcoves, the full upper storey of one of two converted barns, both owned by a gamey old couple, Lew and Ellie Sides. They lived in the bigger of the two barns. To avoid what she called 'unnecessary subliminal subterfuge', Irma Knoll had asked the Sides if she could call them Mom and Pop. They had agreed, mostly because it sounded like a fun thing to do. Irma had pointed out that when it is absolutely inevitable that people are going to lapse into a particular type of relationship, parent–child, brother–sister or whatever, it is best to pre-empt the confusion and tension that this can create by formally acknowledging the bond from the outset.

'Mom and Pop'. That's how Irma had introduced the Sides to Eve and the other post graduate Equality Studies students at the Christmas party she held in her home. They had made their special cocktail, a bucket full of a drink called Lift Off at Cape Canaveral and were doling it out with the enthusiasm of parents. But as time went by and Lift Off at Cape Canaveral took hold, the Sides grew less comfortable with the roles Irma had imposed on them and went around telling everyone that they were not her parents. Exasperated by the reception he was getting, Lew went next door and brought back the family album insisting that Eve and the group should look through it.

'See. Where is she? She's not there. Is she?' he appealed to Eve who ended up spending a lot more time than she wanted to looking at the Sides's family album.

As she walked past their barn with its narrow windows beaming like space-ship portals, Eve slowed down to listen to the music, a swing classic she recognised and tried to name. For a moment or two she lost sight of why she was there, swept along by her parting image of Lew Sides – Pop – standing in the cold December air in his loose fitting dungarees and plaid shirt playing an imaginary ukulele and singing a song no one recognised.

'That's Pop's party piece,' Irma Knoll was telling everyone

between 'goodbyes' and 'thank yous' and 'Merry Christmases'.

The sense of urgency with which she had set out was, by the time she arrived at Irma Knoll's door, little more than a vague apprehension. It was as if the decision to go to Irma's, in itself, had taken the edge off the need she felt to ring Mary Byrne. Between the time she knocked and the time Irma answered the door she considered not mentioning anything about ringing at all.

Irma welcomed her as though she had been waiting for her all day. She led her in, brushing the snow off her shoulders, treating her as she might a person who she was guiding into a surprise party.

'I need to make a phone and I can't find a call.' Eve laughed at her mistake but when she saw that Irma, stern and analytical, was treating it as a key to some much greater need she stopped.

'I know it. This is a night we're going to remember,' Irma announced in one of those voices public figures reserve for addressing crowds at events of great national significance. Eve, already feeling that what she had to offer was inadequate, looked around sensing that the 'we' included someone else. In that same moment, Nancy Alldice, wearing a long elaborately embroidered caftan and trinkety earrings, walked out of the dimly lit dining alcove to her right.

'You mustn't say anything to each other until I get back.' Irma clasped Eve's forearm as she spoke. 'I'm just not comfortable in this' – and between her forefinger and her thumb she held up a piece of the royal blue smock she was wearing, pulling it out and grimacing.

Nancy Alldice and Eve stood smiling at each other while Irma ran the length of the room to the last of the four alcoves.

'How was Christmas?' Nancy asked, still smiling but with less ease.

Eve considered the question more seriously than Nancy had asked it and was slowly preparing an answer when she heard herself say, 'Fine.' She wondered if she should ask Nancy, whom she liked in a way that it wasn't possible to like Irma, the same question but was unable to stop seeing her as Director of Equality Studies. So they stood listening to the scraping sound of coat hangers as Irma pushed clothes up and down a hanging rail. When she emerged, which she did by backing out into the room, making last-minute adjustments to her hair in front of a mirror which neither Eve nor Nancy could see, she was wearing the same royal blue smock.

'I know. I know,' she said as she hurried towards them, exasperated with herself, 'I didn't realise. I just didn't cop that the impulse to change came from a desire to change the way things were going. It was a cowardly impulse.'

The control she had assumed was so absolute that Eve and Nancy, like faceless figures in an audience watched, waiting.

'Now. That phone call?'

Within seconds, Irma had decided that Eve's need to make a phone call was a plea for help. No doubt about it.

Soon she was sitting at the round table in the dining alcove giving an account of Christmas at The Acre, skipping lightly over everything at first and then returning to the beginning, again and again, as if she was systematically peeling layers off the story. Every so often, feeling unentitled to talk at such length about herself she stopped in a startled sort of way, but only for a few seconds. Irma and Nancy were listening with such intense concentration that all responsibility for silence was conveyed directly back to Eve. But at that early stage, Eve was unaware of the effect those silences were having on her. She was swept along by the excitement of telling her story in terms she considered were of her own devising. It made her garrulous. She spoke in gulps and leaps, recklessly swerving from one part to another and then rushing back with armfuls of connecting facts which she haphazardly spilled out to fill the gaps.

When after about a half an hour or so she first started to step outside her story she saw that Nancy's expression was a good deal warmer than Irma's. Irma's mechanical nodding gave Eve the impression that everything she said could be anticipated. This made Eve alter the way she told her story, leading her to go back over some parts of it, yet again, beefing them up. At the same time she was suggesting, with her own clearly stated reactions to what she was saying, the kind of responses she wanted Irma to have. But she made no impact whatsoever. Irma's nods, like a franking machine, went on labelling every-thing Eve said as 'expected', continuing to make her feel that she was helplessly stumbling through a frequently told story.

Eve began to exaggerate elements of her story. As a result Mrs Doyle, initially occupying a particular place in the world because of the choices she made, became the victim of con-spiracy, a captive in The Acre, cruelly duped into supporting the very system which oppressed and degraded her. Irma, whom Eve expected to reveal a preference for the revised Mrs Doyle, remained unmoved and continued to nod at precisely the same pace as she had all along. Even the arrival of Mary Byrne at The Acre didn't touch her in the way Eve thought it ought. It did prompt her to glance momentarily in Nancy's direction. But that was only because Nancy could not control her own reaction and had made an eye contact plea to Irma to relax the listening rules. It was met with a point blank refusal – laced with icy impatience.

Eve's account of Christmas at The Acre did not end where she wanted it to end. As time trickled on there were countless silences, ringing out, like moisture from a damp rag, whatever was left of her story. She filled each of these silences with whatever wandered into her head, the difficulties her sister-in-law experienced at the birth of her daughter, Eugene's mother's hostility, a detailed description of the Christmas present her Aunt Mona gave her, a diary called My Secret Diary with a thong fitting into a clasp for which there was a heart-shaped lock and an ornate gold-coloured key.

In the indeterminate space available to her, Eve had all but lost her way when Irma finally wrapped up with a decisive 'OK.' In the same breath she told Eve that her handling of everything had been 'pretty good – considering'. Then in a more business-like way she began to elaborate on the 'considering' part. The Doyles, she said, with carefully measured reluctance, were 'a family in crisis'. And for a variety of reasons she promised she would 'go into later', Eve had become the repository of all their pain. It was, she said, a measure of Eve's remarkable strength that she had managed to shoulder the burden of that pain for so long.

Eve looked for, but didn't find, an opportunity to respond in the way she always responded to a compliment, accepting and rejecting it in equal measure. There was a loftiness, and a certainty, in Irma's tone which ruled out any kind of round-about response. She was not handing out compliments, she was stating facts. And these facts carried all the weight of accurate judgements based on universal truths. So when she described Mr Doyle as the 'quintessential patriarch', the judgement seemed to pass beyond her and take its place with the other great knowns of the world.

Irma's movements, almost prim when she had first begun to speak, got more extravagant as she fitted the jigsaw pieces of Eve's life history together. She treated her position in her family, the youngest, as particularly revealing. It, combined with her gender, and the fact that she grew up in the shadow of three older brothers 'within the confines of a rigid patriarchal structure', gave Irma all the clues necessary to account for what she referred to as Eve's pain. It was not a term with which Eve identified as the outset, but Irma used it so frequently that it detached itself from the previous meaning it held for her, becoming a coverall term, a way of describing all aspects of her past experience which were not entirely positive.

Once or twice she felt a twinge of disloyalty, while Irma sifted through life at The Acre, but most of the time she was too captivated by the analysis. It seemed capable of explaining everything that went on, illuminating it in a way that she would never have thought possible. And it had a sort of detonating effect, untangling things and making them seem manageable.

When the door bell buzzed at about nine thirty Eve had difficulty hiding her resentment. She was afraid that the new-found grasp she had on her world would not withstand the gaze of other people. She listened, looking blankly through Nancy's affectionate smile, as Irma opened the door and welcomed the Sides. Eve began to panic when it struck her that the conversation would continue where it had left off and she would find herself telling her story to Lew and Ellie Sides, or worse still, Irma might launch into it. But it was soon obvious, even from the casual way Irma sloped back into the room, laughing and joshing with the Sides that the evening was set to continue on a different plane.

The Sides couldn't recall meeting Eve at the Christmas party but made such a sustained effort to place her that she eventually owned up to a description or at least part of a description of someone whom she knew was not her. At that point they backed off, obliquely aware that if they persisted they might have persuaded her to accept in total the identity they were offering. Lew drew a chair away from the table and sat leaning forward with his elbows on his knees and his freckled hands dangling idly. In between funny, laconically told stories about their son Benny's schemes to make money they kept asking if they were intruding.

Eve listened and laughed with Irma and Nancy, darting in behind the scenes whenever she could to take a look at her new perspective on her place in the scheme of things. There was one part of Irma's reading of her situation which, at the time it was being expounded, made startling sense but which, an hour later, she was unable to pin down. It revolved around the idea that Mary Byrne had been an invisible presence at The Acre, a force which down through the years, had greatly influenced the way the family interacted. The only sense in which she was absent, Irma had said, was 'physically' and she plied that word with extra syllables, charging it with a vehemence which Eve found frightening. If the Sides had not been there she would have asked Irma to go through what she had called The Theory of Absent Presences again. But as it was she just drifted away with the memory of a picture in her first school catechism, a small girl dressed in a red cardigan and blue skirt, flanked by a towering white angel. From there she floated down the slipstreams, slowing down to take stock of the random images, the goose wing her mother used as a duster, the nun whose face moved like a scissors when she said the words, 'The Divine Presence', Eugene. Oh God, Eugene, and straight away she turned her attention to the story the Sides were telling in tandem about dancing lessons they had gone to as part of a preparation course for retirement.

It was still snowing at midnight, light powdery snow, almost transparent. Each new layer was skimmed by gusts of wind and brushed into corners where it piled up, white and glistening. Looking down at the translucent greyness of the pavement snow as she walked, Eve's thoughts were only about the snow. It was as though she had become grounded in the present, stepping lightly, wholly absorbed by every detail of the world as she encountered it in that moment. It was all effortless, just sailing along with the Raleigh Reilly playing fields on her left, returned by the snow to the timeless landscape they once were.

On Tuesday, the first day of the second semester, two letters arrived, one from Star and one from Eugene. Star did not refer to the plan they had made to return before the beginning of term. She launched straight into a detailed account of a visiting Ethiopian 'Premier League' basketball player she met with whom she thought she might be in love. He had agreed to undergo hypnosis in an attempt to link into the collective consciousness of the tribe from which he was descended. In her letter Star went out of her way to impress on Eve how lucky she felt she was. There were exclamation marks everywhere and several brackets of 'can you believe it', inserted mid-sentence, emphasising, with near audible breathlessness, this or that aspect of her good fortune. She said she was 'going to run with the project for three weeks, minimum', hopeful that by that stage she would have enough material for an article. He had already disclosed what she felt were 'very significant insights'.

Star enclosed an assignment, due in at the end of the previous semester, asking Eve if she would drop it in for her. This she set out to do on her way over to her first tutorial that morning in the Equality Studies department. In the distance, walking with conspicuous care on the frosted path and unmistakable in her great, big black cape was Irma. Without any hesitation Eve decided to drop in Star's assignment later that day and hurried to catch up with Irma.

'I should have worn my old ski boots. Thought about it. Can't figure why I dropped the idea. How about you? How are you doing?'

Eve was not sure if Irma was asking her how well she was coping with the icy surface or with things generally so she said, 'OK.' Irma then repeated the OK inflecting it to become a question which Eve immediately took as a go ahead.

'Yeah. OK. I got a letter from Eugene. You know,' she paused, 'Eugene.'

'Looks like you want to talk about it.'

'Yeah. But there's not much to say. He either didn't hear what I said to him or has decided to pretend that he didn't. It's like as if nothing happened.'

Irma said nothing but slowed down almost to a standstill and looked on while Eve worked her hand out of her glove. In her folder between Star's assignment and her new A4 block were both letters. She was half way through taking Eugene's out of its envelope when, fussed by the lengthening silence, she handed both envelope and letter to Irma.

'See what I mean.' Eve had intended to sound knowing, but because she spoke hesitantly she only came across as eager. But there was nothing not even the smallest flicker in Irma's expression indicating what Irma's opinion might be. She looked at it for much longer than it ought to have taken her to read it. Eventually Eve came to the conclusion that Irma had finished reading it but continued to gaze at the page while she thought about what she was going to say.

'Would you mind if I held on to this for the morning? Do you feel protective about it? I mean would you wish to have the contents kept private?'

'No. No. Of course not,' Eve said, relieved and at the same time flattered that Irma was so interested in what she had already made up her mind was going to be the final episode in the Eugene saga.

Later in the day as she mulled over the suddenness with which she became the centre of attention in the Equality Studies tutorial that morning she could not recall the exact circumstances under which she had given Eugene's letter to Irma. Her thoughts leapt forward to what followed as a consequence and remained there as she tried to reconcile the mixed feelings she had about it.

The tutorial was well underway before the possibility first crossed Eve's mind that she might be the person whose experiences Irma was weaving into a discussion on the variety of ways the self can be induced to participate in its own subjugation. She let go of that possibility as Irma waded deeper and deeper into theory only to meet it head on again when the discussion returned to Irma's own experiences.

'There are,' she had begun in a very general sort of way, 'numerous disturbing practices in our culture which we tolerate and in some instances even celebrate ritualistically. These rituals with all their distracting trappings can be, and often are, methods by which society induces unsuspecting persons to accept a greatly diminished status and so facilitate an unequal distribution of power.'

Some ten or fifteen minutes later, looking directly at Eve and reducing the pitch of her voice until it became intimate and confessional, she said that she had very recently come in contact with a person who was being lured into accepting the sort of diminished status she was talking about.

Eve, like most of the others in the tutorial, automatically assumed that Irma was referring to one of the Islamic women with whom she was in regular correspondence through Veil, an international support-by-mail group for women living under repressive Islamic regimes. She had referred to their plight so often during the previous semester that everyone lost sight of the fact that the course she was teaching was supposed to focus on the difficulties facing women world-wide in their quest for political reform and not just those living in Islamic countries.

When it became apparent that Irma might be speaking about someone in the tutorial group the atmosphere tightened. Eve, like several others, looked around, hoping that her niggling suspicion that she was the one being talked about, was unfounded. That hope was short lived. Taking the lead from Irma, the others turned their attention on Eve.

Irma held up a bundle of copies of what Eve immediately feared was Eugene's letter. She was busily reassuring herself that Irma would never be so high-handed and insensitive when she remembered her asking if she felt protective about it; did she want its contents kept private? She tried to persuade herself that her reply to that question was given on the clear understanding that Irma wished to discuss the letter with Nancy.

By the time Irma got around to distributing the pages Eve's anxiety had been replaced by anger, which there and then swung to relief when she saw that it was not a copy of Eugene's letter but only of the jeweller's brochure he had enclosed with it.

'This obscene document arrived in the mail today to one of our group.'

The woman nearest to Irma, Blanche Carpenter, turned the page over, unaware that the obscenities to which Irma was drawing their attention were the pictures of engagement rings. Irma spotted her searching and used the opportunity to re-enforce the point she had been making earlier about how some of the most barbaric practices in our culture are passed off as events to be celebrated. Blanche Carpenter nodded an apology as Irma gently implied that her conditioning had precluded her from seeing the engagement rings for what they were.

'A ring is used to lead a bull around. It's the same shape as a dog collar. It's a replica, a smaller version of a foot shackle. And a hand cuff. It is a symbol of subjugation. Accepting one is a ritualistic enactment of a willingness to be led around, shackled and cuffed. We have been conditioned to celebrate this humili-ation, to regard it as a triumph.'

There was a certain amount of unease when Irma told them to note that the precious stones only come with engagement rings. 'They are an inducement,' she warned, 'a payment given in return for a promise to accept the pure unadorned symbol of subjugation,' and here she paused dramatically ' – the wedding ring.'

Eve watched as Dolly Sleuth, a mature student doing a masters in political science twisted her own ring until the three diamonds were out of sight. She struggled with an impulse to explain that Eugene had sent the brochure in a different spirit. She wanted to tell them all that she was not, in any serious sense, under threat or in danger but her attempts to convey this were met with expressions of such sympathy she gave up.

A brief but fascinating history of rings diverted the group's attention from Eve. There were questions, one of which led to a discussion about similar rituals in other cultures. Irma argued that some of the most primitive practices, 'those that directly acknowledge the servitude involved, are preferable to the insidious snaring of women with' – and she held up the brochure – 'expensive diamonds – Trojan horses.' At that point she drew the tutorial to a close, flattered by the reluctance with which most of her students put away their work and prepared to leave.

'Hold it. Hold it right there,' Irma commanded, smiling in an affectionate sort of way.

Everyone came to a standstill, even Elizabeth and Haley, who were already out in the corridor.

'I know I'm speaking for us all when I say thank you to Eve for the opportunity she gave us to explore this complex and worrying subject. And in such a real way too. It's a difficult time for her, but I don't need to tell you that.' Then, after a brief pause, and in a voice warbling with sincerity, she said, 'Thank you Eve.'

Before Eve had a chance to do or say anything she was surrounded by friendly faces. A distant fleeting memory of fainting at mass crossed her mind, blurring as the sensation of regaining consciousness gave way to alarm at being surrounded by so much concern. She was spirited away on a wave of compassion and bundled into a corner of the cafeteria where she sat surrounded by classmates who could not do enough for her. Protesting was no use. It would mean denying that things were as bad as Irma had made them seem. Any form of denial was out of the question. It would be interpreted as an unwillingness to see that she had been through what one of her classmates kept calling a 'pretty frightening experience'. Anyway she didn't want to give the impression that it was all unfounded.

By lunch time the bones of her story were in place and Eve began to see that there was more cause for concern than she had been prepared to admit earlier. She was, as Pearl Short put it, 'being steered into a marriage contract by her family' and while Eugene was not intentionally 'an oppressor' the consequences of his behaviour were oppressive.

While Eve did no more than go along with some of the views on offer, she seized on others, particularly the notion that she was not responsible for the way things had turned out. A good deal of her thinking revolved around keeping that notion in place.

That evening, repeating what one of them had said, she reminded herself that she had, all along, been an unwitting player in a world that had imposed unacceptable responsibilities on her. Consequently she was not accountable. But that was a position she could only reach by thinking it all out carefully. The rest of the time she was as receptive as she always had been to the expectations of the other players in her world, Eugene, her parents, her brothers. As soon as she was off-guard they broke out of the pens in which she had corralled them and trampled across whatever terrain she had managed to mark out for herself.

Eve and three of the others from the tutorial group became regular Friday evening visitors at Nancy and Irma's. The chat always began in a serious vein, politics, environmental issues, whatever, but as the evening flicked by it meandered into the domain of personal experience. Eve kept them posted on the latest developments at The Acre, let them help to draft a reply to Eugene's proposal, laughing uproariously at some of the suggestions they made. They took an avid interest in Mary Byrne and openly competed when it came to ways of uniting her with her father. They organised a garage sale to raise funds when Eve told them that she could not afford to ring Mary Byrne every week as they had suggested.

When the conversation was in full flight and they were all vying for a chance to speak, Irma was inclined to sit back and wait for an opportunity to remind them of how glad she was that she had taken that chance with the engagement ring brochure. All the way through the Christmas vacation she had been worried about how badly the group had been gelling the previous semester. Elizabeth and Haley's dominance was, she argued, though nobody disputed it, a symptom rather than the cause of the poor level of integration. The group needed to be brought together, to find common ground and unite. Here Eve, the source of the obscene document, got the credit – again.

Chapter

10

EVERYTHING IN THE chubby mahogany wardrobe was ship-shape. Crisp white handkerchiefs on the lower shelf to the left, gloves and scarves behind. A selection of ties, twenty, maybe more, hung on a brass tie-rack, paisleys, tartans, tweeds, club stripes, various crests. Mr Doyle stood looking at them, unable to decide which one to wear.

Somewhere in the back of his mind other thoughts were gathering. Mrs Doyle. Bernadette Byrne. Desiré Good. Mary Byrne. Eve. If he could keep them there, out of shooting range, as he had managed to keep them most of the time since Eve went back, then they would, he hoped, eventually lose their ardour.

He put a tartan tie up to his open collar, wondering if he had ever worn it before. It crossed his mind that his memory could be failing. It was a distant crossing, remaining so as he replaced the tie and idly fingered the barkish texture of a sandy-coloured tweed one, breathing through his teeth to avoid the lavatorial whiff of moth balls.

All at once his mind was full of accusations all directed at his tormentors who had mounted a surprise attack, charging towards him screeching like sea birds. He slammed one of the wardrobe doors shut. Within seconds they had regrouped on a different front, lined up like a firing squad. With his mouth tightly shut and his fists ready to burst he faced them down. One by one they backed off, vacating their places to a different group; a group he periodically summoned up for a volley of accusations, even though he had won a decisive victory over them more than a year ago. It was a whiz kid consultancy group which, shortly before he retired, had been hired to conduct a full scale in-house study of management structures. Mr Doyle, himself partly responsible for hiring them, had performed very poorly in several of the Subsidiary Memory Tests.

'SMT results are well below par,' an over-groomed executive had confided to him during lunch. He said nothing. He just let what he would later call the 'jumped-up Johnny-come-lately' talk on, 'dig his own grave as it were'.

At the end of the programme's plenary session that afternoon he set out to 'wipe the floor with him', denouncing in a voice full of derision one of the tests in which participants were asked to state, without checking, the colour of their socks. He argued that it was the sort of thing a man might not necessarily know. 'A fellow might put on his socks in semi darkness.' His colleagues chuckled. 'Or much more likely, he might not have bothered to look at all.' He went through the motions of putting on socks under his desk, looking around at all the attentive faces, skilfully pacing the silence before the punchline. 'He might not have bothered to look at all, might just have put on whatever the wife left out for him.' The young executive laughed with the others, registering that he was contending with a performer; a staunch company man who turned saboteur when things were not going his way.

'It had nothing to do with memory. Nothing at all,' Mr Doyle mumbled as he slipped his index finger under a striped tie, yacht club committee member special, and flicked it straight off the brass rack.

Mrs Doyle, after a fitful night's sleep in Eve's room, had left the house earlier. He heard her reversing down the drive. This time it was meals-on-wheels. Usually it was Mona's depression, a background fact for over thirty years, which, suddenly on the day after New Year's Day, became the great imperative of Mrs Doyle's life. It kept her in Mona's house from early morning to late at night, helping.

From behind his newspaper the previous night he had listened as she chatted animatedly to Mona on the phone. He had to muster every last shard of self control to restrain himself from asking why the hell she needed to ring Mona when she had spent the previous twelve hours with her. But in the changed order of things that would have prompted the scrutinising look Mrs Doyle had perfected, a look which referred everything back to New Year's Day. Then more sanctions would follow.

At the last second, when the conversation with Mona had seemed just about to end, Mrs Doyle revived it. And, charged with this new lease of life, it continued for a further fifteen minutes. She reminded Mona that since she had become the mainstay of the west city meals-on-wheels station with fifty-one regulars on the books, she didn't have a minute to spare. But 'be busy'. That was her motto. And she followed it through with a range of supporting axioms all loudly delivered in Mr Doyle's direction. The devil makes work for idle hands. Duty before pleasure and so forth. Foundering around in his own anger he was not in a position to see that she was, with growing confidence, rowing back through the years, merrily abandoning all the self restraint that it had taken to meet his need for peace and quiet when he was reading the newspaper.

Even though he had formed a very clear picture of her plans for the day and knew beyond doubt that she had left the house early that morning he could not rid himself of the lingering expectation that she was about to appear, her old cheerful self, all set to breathe life into the day. It was a well-worn groove and all the more so when everything in the kitchen was just as it might have been if she was there. Two slices of bread ready and waiting in the toaster. All he had to do was 'Press'. His willow-patterned egg-cup looked as small as ever between his outsized cup and saucer and his side plate. With their faded hunting scenes and worn gold rims Mr Doyle's cup, saucer and plate were familiar almost beyond the point of familiarity, nearing the day when he would pick up one of the pieces and examine it as though he were discovering the hunting sketch for the first time.

'The News'. He padded rapidly over to the radio, reaching to turn it on long before he got near. He was of that generation which sat around wirelesses in the same way as a previous generation sat around pianos. He never got used to listening casually. He claimed he couldn't follow what was being said unless he was sitting down. Consequently his first major target of the day, a target determining a whole series of preceding minor targets, was to be sitting down ready to eat his breakfast before the eight o'clock news pips sounded. He was unwilling to take advice about fine tuning the wireless, preferring the scratchy fuzz, the distant war-time crackle to the whistle-clear voices Anton or Syl could get. When the pips sounded, he scowled with concentration, head tilted waiting for the weighty declaration ... 'This is the eight o'clock news.' It was comforting to feel so directly involved in the greater world. If at that moment, and this was a totally private ritual, a knob of butter was fully melted into the yolk of his boiled egg and his tea poured steaming hot, then all augured well for the day.

With the accusing voices reduced for the most part to thin, faraway plaintive cries, it was turning out to be such a day, things happening with that reassuring precision which he valued as he valued life itself.

He prided himself on how well he had adjusted to retirement. He knew men – busy, active men in their prime – who, as soon as they retired become slouches, limp purposeless fellows pottering about the house in fawn cardigans waiting for hyacinths to shoot, reading the small ads, talking to their wives about their bowel movements. That wasn't for him. No sir. He was determined to fill his days, not choc-a-bloc as they had been for so long but full enough to keep himself on the ball as it were.

A visit to the barber. That was his plan for the morning. And afterwards maybe a quick look in on his former colleagues at Good, Good and Stavely, only a few minutes walk away from the barber's shop.

He fastened his driving gloves, squeezing the right wrist fastener first and then the left. A small adjustment to the rear view mirror and he was on his way. Only once on the seven-mile journey to the city centre, when he saw a white Mini like Mrs Doyle's, did he hear sniper fire again. The rest of the time he was in bouncy good humour, whizzing along a route he had driven so frequently it required no concentration whatsoever.

He didn't have to travel so far to have his hair cut. He could have easily decided to have it cut locally in the newly built shopping mall called The Mall. There was a hairdressing salon there called Hair Sculpture. He had tried it out once – over a year ago when it first opened. Found himself standing, uncharacteristically lost for words, in front of a receptionist with pitch black hair shaped like a Nazi helmet, gently kicking the outer of her crossed legs back and forward.

'Have you got an appointment, sir?' she asked him, flicking the pages of the appointments register with robotic wrist movements.

He glanced at the empty salon.

'Let me see. I think I can fit you in,' she said, a response which became the punch line when, on the first visit back to the office, he recounted the story to Donal at the security desk.

A willowy figure with a jack-in-the-box mop of bouncy curls popped out from behind a curtain, startling Mr Doyle, who quickly withdrew his outstretched arm from the magazines.

With a complicated flurry of gestures he directed Mr Doyle to a bank of washing basins.

'I can tell you're using that hair oil to keep the appearance of colour.'

Overwhelmed by his interest, Mr Doyle raised his hand and began slowly to pat his head as though he were discovering a new part of himself.

'Let's give you over to Sam for a wash and when she's done her bit we can have a good heart-to-heart about the colour prob.'

Mr Doyle who did not intend having his hair washed – who had never had his hair washed in such a public way – was tense and awkward as Sam manoeuvred him into a voluminous salmon-pink smock. It took him a moment or two to get used to the vigour with which she washed his hair, repeatedly digging her fingers into his scalp. Somewhere in his perception of what it should be like, words like caress and stroke were struggling to form. But on the inside track, rapidly outpacing anything else he felt, was irritation. It had mounted to such a pitch that when the stylist reappeared from behind the curtain Mr Doyle blurted out, 'I'm not having my hair dyed, I just want a trim.' He knew it sounded unnecessarily defensive but he didn't care, buoyed along as he was by a whole posse of indignant thoughts. A man can't have things foisted on him like that. Some two bit fly-by-night operation, con artists. What do they take me for? I know a thing or two about commission on cosmetic products. Impudent pup. Fancy boy.

After that he swore he would never have his hair cut by anyone except Jack Scanlon, the barber he had been going to for over forty years.

Edging along bumper to bumper in the familiar morning traffic Mr Doyle became his old combative self again, honking at people who didn't move the instant there was an inch to spare in front of them. He was so preoccupied with schemes to outwit the other motorists, judging the traffic levels at various landmarks and altering his route accordingly, that he lost sight of the purpose of his journey, a hair cut.

He figured that if he could get to the office car park in time he could use one of the younger executive's parking slots, might even teach one of them a lesson about punctuality. It was eight thirty-five. Essential to get in early, to be there ahead of the posse, gives a fellow the edge.

As he drove in the narrow entrance to the car park he found himself thinking once again about what Hugh Thornley had said about him at the retirement dinner. '... the most innovative force in the insurance business, a man who has single handedly brought insurance practice and procedure from its fusty nineteenth-century origins to its present unparalleled levels of efficiency.' Mr Doyle was so moved by what Hugh Thornley said about him that night that he had to cut his thank-you speech short, fearing that his voice might begin to crack and so throw a shadow over a forty year reputation as a solid type, not the sort who goes to pieces just because he hears a flattering profile of his life's work. Here was a man, Hugh Thornley, who, during his ten years as a fellow board member of Good, Good and Stavely, had done everything in his power to find fault with Dick Doyle. Every opinion. Every decision. Extraordinary, to Mr Doyle's way of thinking, that all along Hugh Thornley had held such a high opinion of him ... 'the most innovative force' ... 'single handedly' ... In the same astonished whisper he repeated the phrases every time he watched the video of the occasion, regretting how critical he had been of Hugh Thornley all those years, but at the same time feeling vindicated in his belief that trying to understand other people is a waste of time.

Although only three of the eight spaces in the office car park were occupied, Mr Doyle's choice of slot was effectively restricted to two of the remaining five. The other three were in the board member's zone to the front. He had no difficulty keeping out of that section, recalling how reproachful he used to feel when he saw an unfamiliar car there. The choice was between a slot with the letters AM stencilled on the wall facing it and the one beside it allocated to PL. As he knew PL and did not know AM but reckoned he must be the new personnel manager he decided to park in AM's space. He had no time for what he called 'personnel types', considered them to be generally ineffectual yes-men who didn't know where their bread was buttered. He swung his arm over the passenger seat as he backed into AM's space, then hopped out of the car and headed for the barber.

The last hair cut he had had was just before Christmas, the day of the Good, Good and Stavely party. He had snapped at Mrs Doyle before she had even finished asking him why he needed to go to a barber's shop such a distance away. As he recalled the incident, walking from the car park to Jack Scanlon's, he was gripped by a fit of annoyance, visible to passers-by because of the way he clenched his fist and swung it at an imaginary opponent. Suddenly they were all there again, Bernadette Byrne, Desiré Good, Mrs Doyle, circling around him like rooks, swooping and flapping their black wings as they snapped at his face and pecked his ears and the top of his head. It took more self control than he had not to cower, but somehow he didn't and with Jack Scanlon's in sight he quick-stepped along.

The shop with its ordinary sash window and hall door opening onto the street had originally been the front room, the parlour, of some artisan family. In his fifty years there Jack Scanlon had made few changes. The fireplace, an ornate cast-iron piece with the intricacies of the leafy pattern clogged and caked by a century of paint, stood out in an otherwise featureless room. Barber shop accessories were so few and the furniture, a chair and a bench, so sparse that the whole operation seemed temporary. There were no magazines but Mr Doyle could remember a time when there was an assortment of American magazines, sent by Jack Scanlon's sister in the

Bronx. The only adornment was a cardboard advertisement in the fire grate, a woman with crinkly hair, of a pale omelette colour, smoking a cigarette but momentarily distracted by anyone who looked in her direction. The wallpaper had faded to a point that only the thin burnished gold lines, dividing columns of pale blue violets, revealed anything of the parlour quality of the original pattern. The blackish remains of long rivulets running all the way down from the ceiling in one corner of the room, ended in a grey furry fungus just above the skirting board.

The shop was never formally open or closed. The door frame clanked and rattled whenever anyone tried to open it and if it was locked Jack Scanlon arrived to let them in. In that way the shop opened when the first customer arrived and closed when the last one left.

Although conscious of how shabby the place was, Mr Doyle was not at all critical. He admired the stubborn way Jack Scanlon had resisted all the fads of the past thirty years from crew cuts and Beatle fringes to long locks and punk spikes.

When he arrived at the shop, he pulled the door-knob back and forward rattling the whole frame as if getting in was a matter of life and death. Jack Scanlon's footsteps sounded, rushing towards the door. He opened it as quickly as he could and stood back fastening his collar button and pulling down his rolled-up sleeves as Mr Doyle tumbled in. With his hand shielding his unshaven face Jack Scanlon excused himself, pointing to the door into the living quarters but not managing to say he wanted to get his grey nylon coat. He backed away repeating Mr Doyle's name, assuring him he would be back in a minute.

The cardboard woman with the crinkly hair in the fire grate immediately caught Mr Doyle's attention. Before he could check himself he was telling her that he was being unfairly persecuted. She looked at him vacantly blowing smoke in his face with a callous lack of sympathy.

He looked about the place, calmed by how everything was as it always was, the lino worn through to the concrete in a semi-circle around the cutting chair, and Jack Scanlon never making you dwell on yourself with unmanly talk about style. Discreet too, trimming ear and nose tufts without being asked, without even referring to it.

As he progressed with the job, Jack Scanlon made his way through the usual topics, the weather, boxing – he had been a middle-weight boxer of note in his youth – and changes on the street. He systematically went through a list of the retail premises which had changed hands over the years. It was a routine which Mr Doyle enjoyed.

'At least there's no fear of you lot going,' he said by way of consolation to both himself and Mr Doyle.

'That's true,' Mr Doyle answered, keen to change the subject. He promised himself that some other time he would get around to telling him that he had retired.

He put on his coat and slowly folded the payment into Jack Scanlon's hand, holding it while a grateful Jack Scanlon registered that there was more there than the cutting charge.

'Thanks, Mr Doyle.' But Mr Doyle was not listening, he was staring at the crinkly-haired lady in the fire grate.

'Women,' Mr Doyle announced, offering the world a solution to a problem which had plagued it since its beginning.

'Women,' Jack Scanlon agreed with weary resignation.

At half past nine Mr Doyle was standing outside Jack Scanlon's, wondering if he should visit the office. Just to say hello. He hadn't seen any of them for almost six weeks, not since the Christmas party. He figured that as his car was in the office car park he wouldn't have to make up his mind until he got there.

There was nothing leisurely about his pace, striding along, taking particular pleasure in outpacing men half his age. He didn't stop when he reached the car park, just cut straight across and walked confidently into the office lobby.

'Mr Doyle.' Donal in the security cage looked alarmed.

Mr Doyle treated it as a greeting and raised his whole arm in a salute, his fingers widely splayed. With his head bowed and held close to the upper part of his outstretched arm, like a shot putter, he strode right past. Pretending not to hear Donal calling his name a second time he quickened his pace, determined to catch up with two men ahead of him, their slim thumb-grip briefcases swinging to the side.

All three arrived at the lift together and as they waited, Mr Doyle, brimming with good humour, began to tell a joke about a mermaid who got left on the beach when the tide went out. The lift arrived and Mr Doyle, laughing and nudging his way through the joke, was about to step in when Donal, his voice squeaking with urgency called out from the security cage which he wasn't allowed to leave.

'Mr Doyle, Mr Doyle. The car. It'll have to be moved. Mrs Musgrave had to park over near Bridge Street.'

Mrs Musgrave? Mr Doyle stood with his foot against the lift door keeping it open, confused, racing through the joke, thrown by the suave composure of the younger men who looked quizzically at each other. Then squaring himself up for the punch-line he inadvertently took his foot away and the stainless steel door closed. He stood facing it, almost touching it with his forehead, smiling, absolutely certain that one of them would press the 'open' button to hear the end of the joke.

'Mr Doyle. My life won't be worth living if that car is still there when she goes to get her car from Bridge Street when the disc runs out.

Mr Doyle looked at Donal, who was hanging as far out of the security cage as possible.

'No bother, Donal.' He watched the lift locator light One. Two. Three. Four.

As he backed out of Mrs Musgrave's parking space he reminded himself that he was a member of the board which a decade previously had approved the appointment of the first woman actuary in the business, Helen Harrington. He wondered if Mrs Musgrave knew that. He began to tell her, admitting when she questioned him that he had not personally voted in favour of Helen Harrington's appointment but had, on many occasions – mind you – drawn the attention of the board to the calibre of her work. 'As good as any man's and better in some respects,' he said out loud. He went on to tell Mrs Musgrave that he had even developed a theory on the strength of Helen Harrington's performance: a lone woman in a senior position – not the overall boss, mind – is more highly motivated, more determined to hold her own and so more productive than her male counterparts. He leaned back as he thought about how right he was on that score. He assured Mrs Musgrave that there were, of course, other factors at play. He was not so arrogant as to suppose that it was wholly on the basis of this theory that, during his tenure on the board, almost every department in Good, Good and Stavely, had had a woman appointed to its senior ranks. His theory had played an important part, that's all.

Without having made a decision about it, in the same way as he had made no actual decision to go into the office, Mr Doyle was on his way back to The Acre. Ten o'clock. He would be back by ten thirty. The rest of the day stretched before him, a great empty plain to be crossed. No cover, he would be wide open to attack until sundown. Then he remembered lunch. He had seen it in the fridge before he left, a chicken leg and a few scallions tightly cling-filmed to a Pyrex plate. He found himself wishing things would return to normal at The Acre. Something he could not afford to think. A big mistake, going down that road again. But it was too late. He was surrounded, hemmed in on every side by his tormentors. Without giving them any warning he jammed his foot on the accelerator and forced them out of the way. They leapt to the side and he tore ahead, checking his rear view mirror to see if any of them were following.

Soon he was sailing along the Coast Road, dazzled intermittently by the sunlight bouncing off the silver-papery sea. He began to wonder what Mrs Musgrave looked like but made little progress because before he had a proper opportunity to examine what he had conjured up it had turned into an image of Helen Harrington. Flat chest. Narrow hips. Suspicious of jokes. Now, if Mrs Musgrave had been appointed to head any other department except Personnel, he would have considered it a mistake. But with the personnel nambie-pambies it made no difference. Still it had changed the line-up in the car park.

'Mrs Musgrave.' He said her name with warmth and curiosity, explaining to her, as though she were there beside him, that he got no kick out of taking her parking space. He had begun to reassure himself that like any self-respecting man, he had no wish to inconvenience a woman in that way, when, out of the corner of the rear view mirror, he spotted his tie.

'Holy God,' he gasped aloud.

An army of thoughts swarmed around the relief he felt that he had not gone into the office. It would have been a disaster. He gripped the steering wheel until his driving gloves were about to burst, checking his tie at every opportunity. An outright disaster if he had met Hugh Thornley. The yacht club committee member special, like a red rag to a bull.

'The most innovative force' ... 'single handed'. Hugh Thornley's words stood like a great dam, holding back all that had gone before. Years of hostility, dating back beyond the rawest episode, six or seven years previously, when a vacancy had arisen on the yacht club committee and Dick Doyle had canvassed two fellow committee members not to vote for Hugh Thornley. Everything he had said and a lot more besides found its way back to Hugh Thornley. Accusations were met with counter accusations and before long it was open war. They fought in the board room, they fought in the canteen, they fought in the gents' toilets.

'Tricky enough,' was how Dick Doyle had been describing

his position until Hugh Thornley threatened legal action for defamation. He did not back down for weeks, not until *Yachting Times* carried an article titled 'Wharf War', obliquely fingering Hugh Thornley as the aggressor. As a consequence he was accused by several leading members of bringing the club into disrepute.

To Mr Doyle's incalculable relief Hugh Thornley was not elected to the committee and resigned after delivering a fiery speech about skulduggery and character annihilation. The following weekend he joined an antique automobile club and within the year he was elected president.

From the night of Hugh Thornley's resignation, the episode was never mentioned by either of them, although Dick Doyle could not help flaunting his victory and very occasionally wore his yacht club committee member tie into the office. It never failed to do the trick.

Hugh Thornley's generous speech at the retirement dinner had brought it all to an end. And, not one to bear grudges, as Mr Doyle reminded himself, he was more than pleased that, so aggressively decked out, he had had the cop-on to stay clear of Hugh Thornley.

Mr Doyle got out to open The Acre gates and looked up at the house. Ten thirty-five. Mrs Doyle would not be back for at least twelve hours. Not that her return would make much difference. She would go on punishing him, which was what he believed she was doing by her intolerably long absences from The Acre. He stood looking at the house, taking it in slowly. Before he knew it he had again allowed himself one thought too many about it all, triggering a full-scale daylight attack. An ambush. Unless something very unforeseen happened he could spend another whole day in battle, arguing his case with himself.

His tormentors did not, as he hoped they would, lose their ardour. If anything, they became more resolute and more daring as the months went by, plaguing him on the golf course, in the yacht club bar, during 'The News', everywhere and anywhere. By early summer he was ready to accept any terms if Mrs Doyle would agree to call off the siege. But she appeared to have become almost unrecognisably self-reliant. She came and went at will, often managing to avoid him for days on end. For a long time she continued to do all her household chores, often cleaning and cooking late into the night. Then bit by bit the futility of keeping things spick-and-span began to drain the enthusiasm necessary to keep up the legendary standards she had maintained for thirty-five years.

The depths to which life at The Acre had sunk struck Mr Doyle forcibly, one morning towards the end of April. A tin of salmon stood on the kitchen counter for his lunch. A few inches away was a tin opener. Not in itself very different from some of the other arrangements she had made in the preceding weeks it was, nonetheless, a moment of deep despair; a moment around which all the frustrations and humiliations of the previous months began to cluster until Mr Doyle, unable to put up with it for a moment longer, pounded the counter with his clenched fist. The tin of salmon leapt so high that it landed on its side and rolled on to the ground. He swung his foot at it, but missed. Instantly he swung again, kicking it with such force that it chipped the skirting-board at the far side of the kitchen and began to leak a pinkish coloured oil.

Even if she had wanted to abandon all her household chores at The Acre it is unlikely that Mrs Doyle would have succeeded. She was unable to leave a room untidy. She had also been given advice by Betty Cotter, a distant friend of Mona's, who had approached her at a sale of work on Easter Monday and with no more than a conspiratorial glance and a furtively whispered – 'quick word in your ear' – told her that in the event of a separation – 'God forbid' – she could lose her claim on the family home if she failed to meet her responsibilities there – or if she was the one to leave. As politely as she could Mrs Doyle explained that there was no question of a separation.

Still Betty Cotter's advice lingered and every so often, when her enthusiasm for work, especially unpleasant work like cleaning the toilet, was at a low ebb, it kept her going.

Mrs Doyle had no plan. She was hurt to the quick and anxious at all costs not to put words on what had happened. That was her way of managing the world and even though it wasn't working she could not envisage any other. Betty Cotter had also tried to tell Mrs Doyle something about Mr Doyle's conjugal rights but at that point Mrs Doyle considered that it was well within the bounds of reason to change the subject. She felt exceptionally compromised by having to listen to advice offered by Betty Cotter or any other unattached woman for that matter.

Like Mr Doyle she wished for a return to life as it was before – and that was as far as she got – before. The unspoken remained undefined, occasionally diminishing to a point where she could forget that it happened at all. Her hopes for a return to 'before' were pinned on Eve's arrival. She did not have a particular part lined up for Eve to play. She just felt certain that things would change when she came home and that could only be for the better.

Chapter

11

A POSTCARD ARRIVED from Star in February. A market scene in Addis Ababa but the stamp was Egyptian and the postmark Alexandria. She had crammed every millimetre of it, even the space above the stamp, with short enigmatic phrases and minuscule hieroglyphic drawings. Initially, Eve did not realise that each little symbol had been created to convey some fact or other about Star's lot. She thought they were just decorative, an extension of that vast bibs-and-bobs empire of coloured paper clips, figurines, theme stationery, costume jewellery, lucky charms and the like which bulked Star's world. Eve was looking at the tiny drawing of a car with an X through it, wondering about Star in a general sort of way, when it occurred to her that it was a bid to point out that she was having difficulty getting from place to place. It was more straight-forward than any of the others. A cobweb with a match stick figure – hands and legs outstretched. Her boyfriend's name, Duli, printed inside a cloud with a shining sun peeping out from behind. A cracked egg. A squadron of planes, thin ciphers with a blob in the middle, dropping what could have been parachutists or food supplies on a city.

A second postcard arrived from Star in April. A Klee drawing sent from Vienna, a complete change of tack. Serious. She announced that she would be out of contact for a long time. 'Maybe years,' she wrote. She explained that she was trying to unlearn language in an attempt to reach those areas of her psyche as they had been before they became 'colonised by words'. When Eve told Irma and Nancy about it they were intrigued. The Friday group which had taken to meeting at lunch time on Wednesdays as well, though not as religiously, spent the best part of an hour debating whether or not it was possible for someone as verbal as Star to reach her pre-verbal self by the route she had proposed. Irma questioned the notion of an intact pre-verbal self existing separately from the self the individual had become and flatly argued that it was impossible to untangle the interactive relationship between language and experience. It was one of the few times that semester when discussion did not focus on Mary Byrne and the Doyles. In many ways it was a relief to Eve because by that stage, even though she rang Mary Byrne every week, there just wasn't always something to report to the group.

Earlier on in the year there had been a new development to relate after each call. Eve had often felt as though she was ringing for the very first time, forced by Mary Byrne's timidity to start all over again, persuading her that contacting her, their, father was not, as Mary kept saying, the biggest mistake of her life.

Over the months that followed, Eve battled with doubts about her ability to keep Mary on course. She felt she was failing to give her the level of support she needed and had it not been for the encouragement of the Friday group she might easily have been overwhelmed by a sense of failure. Equally she might have lost sight of why she was so involved if they had not been there to remind her of her responsibility to her step sister. But the main focus of their analysis was on the consequences, the grave consequences, for both Mary Byrne and Eve, of backing off. They warned that Mary might well be destroyed if she did not challenge the open rejection she had suffered on New Year's Day.

Irma, pointing out the complexities of behaviour, during a Wednesday lunch in early March, explained that it was likely that Mary had unwittingly participated in bringing that rejection about, thereby validating a life pattern of being rejected.

'Mary needs help to break the rejection pattern. Withholding that help – regardless of how she feels about it – would be a criminal act.'

There were other hurdles to be overcome. Some of these, like Mary's mother's discovery of the attempted link-up, prompted a reappraisal of tactics. Bernadette, who was told by Desiré Good, was inconsolably upset and most of the Friday group agreed that this new development required careful handling. They advised her to work at bringing Mary around to the idea that this was an adventure she and her mother could embark on together.

'Make it sound exciting,' Nancy urged, demonstrating the sort of feeling Eve should generate in Mary until she spotted Irma's lack of enthusiasm. Irma did not say anything but she may as well have told her to shut up. Either way Irma had cleared the decks for her own delivery.

She disclosed her reservations as if she was revealing the details of a plot she had uncovered which posed a serious threat to the lives of the small group gathered around her. She argued that implicit in Mr Doyle's financial support of Bernadette Byrne was the understanding, it may even have been explicitly stated, that she would lead a covert life, a life of shame. She warned Eve of the dangers of inadvertently becoming her father's accomplice by allowing Bernadette Byrne's humiliating bond with him to colour the advice she was offering to Mary.

Eve nodded rhythmically, but only because Irma was speaking so directly to her. She already had the picture and knew the steps she wanted to take to win Mr Doyle's acceptance of

Mary. It wasn't a complicated scheme, just a series of gently paced discussions on issues distantly related to rejection, gauged to bring Mr Doyle around step by step to Mary's point of view. Eve knew the territory well. She had often seen her mother coax and cajole. The secret of handling men, as Mrs Doyle had often advised, was to approach them sideways.

Mary, who had reluctantly gone along with the approach Eve had proposed at the beginning, became more and more enthusiastic and by early May she was actively involved, revising some of the strategies, tailoring them to suit the pace at which she herself wished to approach Mr Doyle. Then, at the end of May, without warning Mary made a determined bid to call a halt to the whole thing. It wasn't worth the bother, she didn't care, wanted to get on with her life, look forward not back. If it had happened in February or even March Eve would probably have agreed but by then she was so well schooled in the behavioural pattern of the rejected that she took a very firm stance and confidently talked Mary through the consequences of such a line of action.

As well as the concern she felt for Mary's welfare, Eve had a definite view of how, by her very existence, Mary had shaped life at The Acre and was, as a result, an unseen influence on her own development. The Friday group had warned her that her own quest for self realisation would be doomed if she allowed Mary, 'the key to the Doyles' disfunctionality', to slip back into the woodwork.

Very occasionally, and not until at least a decade later, would Eve find herself speculating about what might have happened if things had taken a different course.

She tried to picture herself with a life other than the one she had, but never succeeded for more than a minute or two. Any of those imaginary steps she took down other roads led back to precisely where she already was – her apartment or her office, wherever. If she stopped to think about it, which she rarely did, she supposed that the reason why she always worked her way back to the life she had was because it was the one she wanted. Not that there was ever any question in her mind about that. She had made choices, rational well-informed choices which protected her from looking with anything but vague curiosity at other people's lives. One thing she had always been certain about was that she did not want to go down the same road as her mother. She saw it as a profoundly compromised existence, one of servitude, despite the comfort of The Acre. It wasn't the actual circumstances of her mother's life which she found objectionable. These, she knew, were not written in stone. It was the belief that it did not, in effect, amount to a life at all. Many of the steps Eve had taken were to avoid that fate. By choosing consciously and carefully as she had done, she ruled out regret and its ugly sisters, envy and resentment.

Earlier on, during the whirlwind years following her return from Raleigh Reilly, there had not been time even for the smallest amount of speculation. Every minute of every day was swallowed up by what she and everyone in her orbit called 'the enquiry' – a state-sponsored investigation aimed at building a profile of the workforce in the South and South West. After a little over a year its scope was extended and it became a nation-wide study. The project director found herself too tied up by other commitments to undertake the extra work involved and her recommendation that Eve be appointed in her place was duly accepted.

As head of the newly expanded research team, Eve took the step – much lauded by a wide range of interest groups – of redefining the terms of the report. 'Educational achievement' remained as it was: the level of formal education reached by each individual participating in the enquiry. But 'the work they carry out' was expanded from its original narrow definition as 'work carried out in formal work settings' to include casual and part-time work and, more controversially work carried out by women in the home. The report, referred to as the Doyle Report to the amusement of Anton and Syl, would probably have met the same fate as the great bulk of reports had it not become the basis for the funding of a variety of projects aimed at correcting gender imbalances. Eve was appointed the over-all co-ordinator of these projects with responsibility for funding. In that way it came about that work carried out in the home, because it was categorised as part of the service industry, became in some instances eligible for grants to improve productivity.

Mrs Doyle could not help hoping, even after a decade, that all this was a phase, a prelude to settling down. It was not a hope she owned up to or even hinted at. She had thrown herself into Eve's world that hot June afternoon Eve arrived home from Raleigh Reilly and had, without intending to, remained there ever since.

It was a matter of pride to Mrs Doyle that she had never suffered the indignity of having to take responsibility for herself. So independence was a climb down and on some occasions a humiliation. That it had taken its toll was immediately obvious to Eve when she saw her mother at the arrivals gate. Mrs Doyle looked drained. She had a vagueness about her, so unfamiliar that Eve, forgetting how she might respond, intoned her 'how are you' with meaning.

'Great. I'm fine. Never better. How are you? You look smashing.'

When Eve asked her if she was sure, she seemed puzzled and looked over her shoulder as though searching for someone to confirm that the answer she had given was correct. Eve was pushed to the limit trying to link the view of her mother's circumstances she had worked out at Raleigh Reilly to the person who had come to collect her at the airport. Somehow Mrs Doyle seemed to be getting away with her own version of herself. Applying the strategies she had devised to help her mother change her outlook suddenly seemed a long way down the line.

Eve had imagined that once outside Mr Doyle's orbit, her mother would discover a world full of possibilities. She would get the opportunity to reclaim herself after all those years servicing the needs of others. Perhaps if Mrs Doyle had voluntarily stepped outside that orbit then there would have been some basis for Eve's expectations. But Mrs Doyle had been pushed by the unnameable event and was finding it very difficult to manage. It was not that she had ever wanted Mr Doyle on hand all the time. It was just that she had seen the world through his eyes for so long that she saw only what he saw. She had always been too busy anticipating his responses to give her own any serious consideration. It was some time before Eve worked out that her mother did so even when Mr Doyle wasn't there. Forced to keep him out of her mind by what she hoped she would never to have to name, every experience, even meeting Eve at the airport, had a raw unfiltered texture to it. She knew women who were permanently in a similar position, forced to make decisions and tackle the world head on and had always considered their lot lamentable and in one or two instances, tragic.

Over and over again she told Eve how relieved she was to see her. Then she just stood there waiting for Eve to decide when they should start making their way to the car park. She handed Eve the car keys in the way a small child might offer something dangerous, scissors or a box of matches, to a parent. On the way out Mrs Doyle stuck close by Eve's side, ready to stop when Eve stopped and inclined to move right in, shoulder to shoulder, when it seemed as though someone might momentarily divide them.

It would not have been so awkward if she had had a plan, but she didn't. She just believed that once Eve came home life at The Acre would somehow return to normal and that the events of the previous winter would fade into the background,

148

then disappear altogether. She believed this as she believed that a well set table or a clean house was a defence against adversity.

Initially her childlike dependence frightened Eve who, though completely committed to setting things to rights, felt her confidence drain away. She had to keep reminding herself that there would be no hope of making progress if she just let herself be drawn headlong into her mother's distress. At the same time she found it virtually impossible to step back far enough to offer the sort of advice she knew, at least in theory, would help. She was continually disarmed by the way her mother looked at her when she tried, even in the most tentative way, to speak objectively about what was happening.

She thought about Elizabeth and Haley and about how the Friday group were forever despairing about the prospect of breaking their interdependence pattern, which Irma said was so extreme that in the case of Elizabeth's death, Haley's chances of surviving more than a few days were negligible. Irma's description had seemed like an exaggeration when Eve first heard it and while she still considered that to be the case she began to look on it as an apt metaphor. Eve smiled when she recalled the vehemence with which Irma had declared that 'the whole thing is a damned sight easier for men, they just step on well worn separation paths and fake it 'til they make it – which in most cases is never'.

Mrs Doyle's flexibility, her infinite flexibility, never annoyed Eve as much as it did that afternoon. On seeing how pleased Eve was when she agreed with her she began to agree whole-heartedly with everything. She agreed before Eve was half way through whatever it was she was saying – or sometimes when she had just begun. The random way she chipped in a 'yes' or an 'of course' or a 'definitely' made it patently clear to Eve that her mother wasn't taking anything she was saying on board. And to make matters worse, Mrs Doyle was behaving as if there wasn't anything wrong with that. On the contrary, she was

delighted with her performance. Eve felt herself sliding helplessly towards exasperation. Familiar territory whenever she
tried to speak to her mother; territory she made one last ditch
effort to avoid.

'You don't have to agree with everything I say.'

Mrs Doyle was offended but at the same time made up her
mind to try and disagree and from then on offered a careful
balance of agreement and disagreement in response to everything Eve said.

They were almost at The Acre when it struck Eve that her
mother, whether intentionally or not had dictated the terms
of their conversation. Mary Byrne's name had not been mentioned. Eve had referred to her, but in such an oblique way
that both of them could easily have imagined that it wasn't a
reference at all. Eve's frustration, evident in jerky gestures, side
glances at her mother and impatience with other motorists,
reached a new pitch outside The Acre when she pulled the
hand brake with such force that she elbowed Mrs Doyle in the
thigh.

'What about Mary Byrne?' Eve had not allowed herself to
think about the question before she asked it. It followed so
closely on the realisation that she was being manipulated into
denial that it was accusative and to Mrs Doyle's way of thinking
very aggressive. Still, she proceeded to get out of the car as
though what Eve had said was just by-the-way. There was
nothing, not a single grimace or gesture which revealed that
she had heard the question. Mrs Doyle checked herself in the
mirror and carefully palmed the surface of her hair, treading
one or two stray hairs back into the main bulk.

'One of these days I'm just going to let it go grey. I don't
mean like the old woman of the roads. God be between us and
all harm. Something between ashen and silver. What do you
think?'

Contrary to all Eve's plans she grabbed her mother by the
arm.

'I said, what about Mary Byrne?'

The muscles that kept Mrs Doyle's expression pleasant, like the all the ropes and pulleys that keep an elaborate stage set in place, began to quiver. By pressing her lips firmly against one another she tightened her whole face and then held it in a fixed expression, an all-out attempt to sustain pleasantness. But within seconds it had snapped, leaving her unrecognisably deflated, her face slack and sprawling like a collapsed marquee.

Her words, when they eventually surfaced, sounded guttural and eerie. Many were distorted by gulps for breath or lost altogether, choked before they surfaced. Mrs Doyle was not weeping or crying but baying with all the pathos of a mourner. Eve gripped the steering wheel so tightly that the skin on her knuckles took on a porcelain-like sheen. She was certain she was going to lose the battle, that her guilt at removing the scaffolding which kept her mother's world in place would get the upper hand and she would be forced to backtrack into pretence and denial. What saved her, though only barely, from that fate was a particular Friday group discussion, led by Irma, on how difficult it is for a daughter to withhold assent from a mother. Irma said it was the great stumbling block, the one that brought even the most resolute to their knees. But she said that those who withheld assent for the right reasons are frequently rewarded by the sight of their mothers following them into what Irma conjured up as the promised land, the domain of reason and choice.

Despite the odds, and probably because she was so familiar with her mother's way of thinking, Eve got the drift of what she was trying to say. From among that vast jumble of words and half words Eve selected and joined together three key pieces of the jigsaw. Mary Byrne. Eugene Wall. September wedding.

All Eve's resources went into consoling her mother who plunged deeper and deeper into despair, hitting previously uncharted levels of devastation as the scale of the tragedy came fully into her line of vision. Up until then it had remained unexplored, cordoned off like the scene of an accident. So it was there in the passenger seat of her white Mini facing the garage doors of The Acre with Eve in the driving seat, that the full impact of Eugene Wall's impending marriage to Mary Byrne together with all the consequences, hit Mrs Doyle for the first time.

Eve put her arm around her mother's shoulder and grasped her hand, stalling as she contained her fright at how limp and cold that hand was. Slowly she began to work her way towards a vantage point from which both of them could look at what had happened. Mrs Doyle, despite the heat of the afternoon, was shivering. Eve suggested they go inside but that only prompted a new wave of tears, this time a low sustained whimper in which Mr Doyle or Daddy cropped up every few seconds.

Eve was at pains to resist the impulse she had to offer Mrs Doyle a complete clinical rundown of her situation. It would, she knew, be neither fair nor constructive and would almost certainly be hurtful. Even with those resources like restraint and tolerance, fully on tap, bits of that rundown still broke loose and found their way into the conversation. When she heard her mother call Mr Doyle 'Daddy' for the fifth or sixth time she was unable to contain her reaction.

'For God's sake stop calling him Daddy, he's not your father.'

Mrs Doyle laughed but only because she thought that was what she was supposed to do. When she discovered it wasn't she began to cry again.

'I can't go in looking like this.' She examined her ravaged face in the mirror.

'Look,' Eve said, sorry she had spoken so forcibly and assuming command in a way she had not done until then. 'We'll go for a drive.'

Mrs Doyle sat up in her seat. 'Yes. A drive and then we'll go to Mona's. I can ring the hairdresser's from there.'

Inside, pacing up and down in front of the bay window like a caged panther, Mr Doyle was restraining himself from going out and asking them what the hell they were talking about. But he knew full well that things had changed and might change even more. He listened, incredulous, as the car started up and then looked on in glazed bewilderment as it drove out on to the estuary road. Soon he was wrapped in self pity, seeing himself as the victim of yet another unprovoked attack. He looked around the room, fixing on the big spread of newspapers on the floor, weeks of news with a glass – tawny dregs and a froth-crusted rim – sitting on top.

Desperate for a cease-fire, he began to play with the idea of compromise. He pawed it this way and that, as a cat might play with a mouse, confident that at any moment he could deal it a death blow.

Later he returned to it again and began, as he had done earlier, to toss it about idly, all the time looking at the disarray in the room. He made no attempt to resist the pace at which the idea was growing in appeal.

This had not come about through a change of heart, though to the other players that might well have appeared to be the case. And it didn't spring from a belief, or even an distant inkling, that he might, in some way have contributed to the plight in which he found himself. It became possible because while he dallied with the notion he began to imagine that it was Mrs Doyle's idea. It had all the hallmarks of her thinking, even presenting itself in that speculative way she had of offering her opinion. The loose scatty way it took shape and the endless revisions it underwent as he mulled it over left Mr Doyle with little choice but to attribute it to Mrs Doyle.

So when Eve rang him from Mona's she was disarmed, first by his good humour and the open affectionate way he welcomed her home and then by the lack of resistance he put up to the mediating role she was taking on. He told her that Mrs Doyle had not been herself for some months, not herself at all. He showed a willingness, beyond all expectation, to go along with every suggestion Eve made. Between them, he implied, they would get her back on her feet – whatever it took. When Eve had mentioned Mary Byrne's name and by inference her plight, her father was sympathetic but managed to make it seem like a side issue. Soon he was chatting about Eve's term papers, prospective grades, jobs, opportunities, contacts, angles. She said she would be over later, once they had 'settled Mona in for the night'. He told her he was just about to leave for the yacht club but would be in well before eleven.

However wide the gap between Mrs Doyle as she was conjured up by Eve in Raleigh Reilly and Mrs Doyle as she appeared at the airport that afternoon, there was an even wider gap between Mr Doyle the oppressor and the man who listened eagerly to everything she had to say when she spoke to him from Mona's.

The fact that the Friday group were meeting as always had been playing on Eve's mind all evening. She wished she were with them and in a spirit of conscious self indulgence allowed herself to experience fully the loss she felt whenever a newly remembered detail of the Friday evenings struck her. Even a momentary recollection of the gingham tablecloth was enough to intensify the longing to be back. She was recalling the way Irma insisted on going over the pizza order five or six times when she decided to ring them.

Mona shivered at the words 'short transatlantic call', before assuring Eve that she didn't have to ask. Then with a tight spicy smile and a single coy nod she managed to insinuate a guess that there was romance involved.

As well as the fun of just talking to the Friday group, Eve felt certain that they would be able to help her deal with the confusion brought on by trying to bridge the gap between her differing versions of her parents.

At first she thought they had all had a lot more wine to drink than usual and began to calculate the time differential again, imagining that it must be later there than she thought. Several voices came down the line at once with Nancy's voice sounding marginally louder than the rest.

'I can't believe it. It's telepathic serendipity.'

The others, Janice Bird, Pearl Short, Dolly Sleuth, like a chorus in a musical, were taking turns to yell 'surprise'. Then all in a flurry, with no one voice distinguishable from the others, 'Let Irma tell her herself. Let Irma tell her.' Sudden silence.

'Hello Eve. Eve. Are you there? Hell, for a minute I thought it was some sort of hoax. This is' – and Irma stayed poised on the *is* while she searched for a word to convey her amazement. 'I mean you calling right now. Nancy and I have just told the others, right now, about our plan to spend part of our vacation in Ireland. It was going to be two weeks in London. You knew that didn't you? The Veil conference. Then we got thinking. The conference, one week. Right? Five days to be exact. It's not part of the deal – I mean going to Ireland isn't part of the deal – so we'll have to make our own reservations. Hotels. Maybe you could help?'

'Sure.'

'It'll be three days. Three days in Cork,' her voice grew distant as she turned to check the itinerary with Nancy. 'Let me see. Right here. Three days, beginning July second. And then Killarney, Galway and Dublin. One overnight in each. How does that sound to you?'

'Fine. I mean that's great.'

'Now. How have you been?'

'Things have changed here.'

'Like how?'

'Like Mary Byrne and Eugene Wall are getting married in September and my mother is treating it like a death in the family.'

'Right.' Irma stopped to think but held the gap in the conversation by clicking her tongue rapidly, sending what seemed like Morse code signals down the line. Then the word 'inevitable' followed, taking Eve completely by surprise.

'Inevitable?'

'Sure. He's exploiting,' and here Nancy changed tack. 'The point is how do you feel about it.'

'OK, I think. I mean I'm glad he's out of my hair.'

'Look, don't say anything else. Can you keep it under wraps 'til I get there and we'll … you need to think about putting something in place to sort it all out. I mean the whole thing with your family. All that denial and deception and the level of control necessary to contain it.'

Eve heard Mona and her mother whispering outside the half opened door. The level of tension Mona was exuding about the cost of the call forced Eve to try and wind it up which Irma treated as an attempt to avoid confronting the facts of her life.

'Why don't you bring everybody together and at least give them some of the language to understand what's going on?'

'That's a lot easier said than done.' Eve found herself thinking about a picture in a book she had when she was very young; a group of mice with little blue hats listening to an orator mouse who had just suggested putting a bell on the cat.

'Look. I know the details. Set aside an afternoon. July third or fourth. I'll help. You know – set up an infrastructure. Define the terms. And everyone can progress from there.'

Eve's first reaction was to say no but as she tried to think of an effective way of turning down the offer, she suddenly found herself in the grip of an impulse to say yes. The claustrophobia she felt in that dark brown room with her mother and Aunt Mona whispering at the door were the deciding factors. Irma was like a breath of fresh air. Agreeing to let her organise an across-the-board reconciliation was a rejection of all the subterfuge that went on in the doorways of dark sitting rooms, all the dehydrated lives that were lived out in houses like her Aunt Mona's with its highly polished brasses and towering monkey puzzle tree in the garden. Besides, Eve was beginning to have serious doubts about her ability to make headway alone. Her attempt earlier on to explain to her mother, that even if Mary Byrne had never existed she still had no intention of marrying Eugene Wall, was in vain. The mere mention of their names was enough to set off a new bout of lamentation.

Mrs Doyle was in spectacularly good form that evening. It sometimes appeared to Eve as though her mother was offering high spirits and immeasurable compliance in return for no discussion on the key issues. But even that immeasurable compliance began to seem suspicious. Every time she said they ought to leave for The Acre, Mrs Doyle, agreeing whole-heartedly, stood up – but somehow after a few minutes managed to be sitting down again. Eventually, when Eve decided to go to The Acre by herself, Mrs Doyle agreed with the plan in the same fulsome way that she had been agreeing to go there herself for over an hour. It did not emerge till later that Mrs Doyle had, in fact, moved in with Mona and had only been back to The Acre twice in the previous six weeks. She found it impossible to go there but she also found it impossible to say so.

Mr Doyle was still at the yacht club when Eve arrived at The Acre. A special meeting of the committee had been called late that Friday night to deal with the arrival the following day of forty-two members of the Hong Kong Wanchai Yacht Club. When he had outlined the twinning scheme to his fellow committee members before he and Mrs Doyle went on the retirement cruise, Mr Doyle had not mentioned the matter of reciprocal membership. It had seemed unimportant at the time, a gesture made in the spirit of twinning. It never occurred to him that the Wanchai Club would regard it in any other light. But the only sense in which members of the Wanchai Club saw honorary membership was literally. That was the whole attraction of twinning. It entitled them to use the facilities of another club which in this instance included participating in a forthcoming annual regatta, an event regularly covered in the international yachting press. The letter announcing their arrival, which came earlier that week, emphasised how much they were looking forward to that week-long event.

When challenged by the committee Mr Doyle skilfully defended his position but denied that he had been responsible for making them honorary members. He survived the calls for his resignation that night but the following day, when the group arrived from Hong Kong, all permanently smiling, delighted in such a polite way to be there, Mr Doyle knew his days on the committee were numbered.

Eve knew that her father was not yet back from the yacht club the minute she drove in the front gates of The Acre that Friday night. The first thought that crossed her mind when she opened the front door was that the house had been robbed. There was an open telephone directory on the hall floor. When she went to pick it up she found that it was stuck to the floor with congealed ball point ink – the burst tube of which reinforced the bond between the directory and the parquet floor. She picked up a cup from the hall stand intending to bring it with her to the kitchen but let go of it when she saw the ermine-tinged fungus rising like a cactus from the dregs at the bottom. It broke when it hit the floor but more or less kept its shape, held together by the fungus.

The smell was so different from the usual mix of lavender wax polish and warm almondy baking that Eve could not identify it. She went over to the holy water font and smelled the water even though she knew that it was very unlikely to be the source of so putrid a smell. She walked towards the kitchen and was about to turn the handle when she sensed that there was someone standing behind her. In the second or two it took to summon the courage to turn around she had entered that domain of fear where even the most familiar places are terrifying. She walked calmly to the front door and, once outside, ran to the car.

She drove along the estuary road with the window fully open. The moist night air billowed around the car, sweeping Mrs Doyle's bridge cards off the dashboard and scattering them all over the back seat. But the sickly smell of something decomposing stayed with her, forcing her to go on witnessing the squalid condition of The Acre and thwarting every attempt she made to regain the distance from which she had viewed it all as her plane touched down earlier that day.

In the days that followed, Eve lost sight of the reservations she had had about letting Irma get involved and began to look forward to her arrival, confident that she was going to play a key role in sorting things out. Irma herself was taking that role very seriously. She rang Eve almost every day looking for biographical details of all the people involved. Sometimes she asked questions that Eve found laughable. Was Mrs Doyle's marriage to Mr Doyle her first marriage? Had there been conflict in coming to a decision about family size? Was sexual attraction an obvious feature of their marriage prior to the appearance of Mary Byrne?

Eve was afraid that Irma's enthusiasm would wane if she told her that Anton and Syl had refused point blank to have anything to do with what Eve had described to them as a family conference. They had both insisted that their parents were well capable of sorting things out themselves and laughed when Eve tried to say that Mary Byrne had been an unseen presence at The Acre for the past twenty-two years. Syl, and to a lesser extent Anton, conveyed a thinly disguised regard for the way their father had handled the whole business. To impress this point on Eve, Syl added up the amount of money he figured Mr Doyle had given Bernadette Byrne and was beginning to adjust the total to take inflation into account when Eve unceremoniously gave in. Noel had agreed to come but predictably insisted that he be allowed to bring his new family with him. Eve settled for one – The Saint – whom she could rely on to say nothing, just as he had done on Christmas Day.

The full extent of Mr Doyle's wish for a return to normal was not apparent to Eve in any of her conversations with him. Mrs Doyle's well being was nearly always the central issue, the only issue as far as he was concerned, and he said he didn't care what it took – conferences, doctors or whatever – he would go along with it. He had persuaded Eve to remain at Mona's until Mrs Doyle chose to return home. This he tactfully implied would happen as soon as she began to recover, an unlikely development if she were left alone with Mona. It only dawned on Eve slowly that he had been using 'unwell' and 'not herself' euphemistically, that the implication was depression. And the source – her own family. He did not go so far as to say, as he had in the past said about Mona, that 'it came with the breed'. He resisted all efforts Eve made to explain that there was a specific reason for her behaviour. The fact that Mrs Doyle herself was unwilling to identify that reason had much further reaching consequences than Eve envisaged at the outset.

Still, when details of the conference began to emerge he managed to change tack, as he would again before the event took place, and began to approach it as he had approached negotiations with the union reps down through the years at Good, Good and Stavely. He said that as far as he could see everyone attending had a lieutenant which entitled him to select one. His choice was Art Wright, the Doyle's family doctor, whom Eve had always regarded as a kind benevolent man.

Mr Doyle did not mention depression to Art Wright. He claimed that the whole thing was a set up, a conspiracy orchestrated by Bernadette Byrne and Desiré Good to make him continue paying maintenance. It should have stopped when Mary, whom he called 'the child' was sixteen. But because 'she took it into her head to go to university' they had got him to go on supporting them until she was twenty-one. Now they had a new set of demands.

160

Irma advised Eve to get everyone as involved in the arrangements as possible. The more they participated in the preparatory stages, Irma said, the more they would stand to benefit from the session. She told Eve that it was only a starting point, an opportunity for all concerned to learn a language that would help them out of the mess into which they had got themselves.

The first word Eve said when she rang Mary was 'congratulations'. And every time Mary went to speak, Eve said it again. The high-pitched excitement with which she enthused about Mary's engagement triggered a spate of 'thanks' and 'thanks-a-million' which continued long after Eve had stopped congratulating her. So when Eve told her about the conference she said 'thanks' and then 'thanks-a-million'. They had talked so much and with such intensity about the importance of a general get-together during the preceding few months, that with an actual date firmly lined up, there was very little left to say, so Eve said 'congratulations' again. And Mary said 'thanks-a-million'. The call ended on a less satisfactory note than any of the calls Eve had made to Mary from Raleigh Reilly. As she mulled this over Eve reassured herself of how appropriate it was to wish Mary well. If she didn't want to be involved with Eugene, which she definitely didn't, then it followed that he was free to be involved with whomever he liked. Mrs Doyle wept whenever Eve pointed this out to her. She was certain that it was a deeply flawed line of argument, but felt unable to expose it as such.

Mrs Doyle spoke of Irma and Nancy as though she had known them all her life. Her belief in Irma's ability to undo what happened over the past six months was absolute. It replaced, without trace, her faith, not a particularly fervent one in recent years, in St Joseph of Cupertino. She had prayed to him on and off in the preceding months but her prayers had gone unanswered. In some ways it was almost as if she welcomed his failure to help. It allowed her to transfer her allegiance to a new icon.

As part of the scheme to get everyone involved, Eve asked her mother if she would make hotel reservations for Irma and Nancy for their three nights in Cork. She did not bat an eyelid when Eve spelled out the unorthodox details of the accommodation they required. Eve felt that this was progress on her mother's part, a definite step out of the oppressively conventional life in which she had been trapped for so long. It did not occur to Eve that it could be a step in the opposite direction, a new level of flexibility. She was not there when Mrs Doyle rang The Alhambra Hotel and was saved witnessing how awkwardly her mother wore the mantle of liberation.

As soon as the phone was answered Mrs Doyle began to give the background to her request for a double room for Irma and Nancy. Intent on getting it right, she continued to sketch the background, working her way to her first question.

'What I rang to ask is if you take gays?'

The gap that followed was so long that Mrs Doyle got the impression that she had lost contact with the person at the other end of the line.

'Hello.'

'Hello.'

'I was ringing to ask if you take gays?'

'There isn't, I mean I don't think there's a policy about...'

'They're very good friends of my daughter's. One of them is a professor.'

'Usually it wouldn't,' and the voice lost confidence. 'Hold on, I'll check.'

Several minutes and a lot of clicking sounds later, a different voice, male, came on the line. Mrs Doyle began to feel that she had gone about it in the wrong way and was anxious to make amends. She started at the beginning, telling the whole story in, what she repeatedly interrupted herself to call, a nutshell. But because she was on new terrain she kept adding bits of information – Eve's scholarship to Raleigh Reilly, her worries about her marrying an American and so on. Bit by bit she was tying herself up in knots, trying to explain something she did not, in the first place, fully understand herself. Every time she said the word conference it sounded more and more like a rally. Eventually she agreed that Irma and Nancy might be happier in a city-centre hotel with easier access to the services they might require for what he had come to regard as their campaign.

'Fine,' Mrs Doyle said efficiently, determined not to say thank you.

Straight away she rang The Monte Casino Palace and booked a double room under the name of Irma Knoll. No complications. She couldn't wait until Eve got home to tell her about the Alhambra's refusal to give Irma and Nancy a room. She had picked up that it was the sort of thing Eve would be interested in hearing. Mrs Doyle was very satisfied with the outcome, as she always was when she indulged any of the many phases her children had gone through over the years. But she was unnerved by the suspicion with which Eve listened to her account of the hotel's refusal to reserve a room for Irma and Nancy. Eve was not at all convinced and had raised her eyes at her mother's attempt to inject the word 'management' with disdain. Still she went along with it as she had gone along with all her mother's attempts to earn a place in her world since she came home.

Chapter

12

EVE COULD NOT believe how like the other passengers Irma and Nancy looked, all belted up in their mackintoshes as if they were expecting rain. For a moment or two she was gripped by the thought that these two women were people she didn't know at all. It was as if the thought had broken loose from all her other thoughts and was setting itself up in opposition, gathering evidence to support the feeling that she no longer wanted Irma to be involved. Wrestling with the feeling that she was being disloyal to her family and at the same time very anxious that it would not be apparent she threw herself into Irma's open arms and stood while Irma patted her back – light rhythmic patting as though Eve had been bereaved.

'We've been so worried about you.' Irma released Eve and smiled as she watched her walk towards Nancy, unsure of how she should greet her. Then, with Nancy's mackintosh shoulder buckle pressing into her chin, Eve asked them what kind of flight they'd had.

'We didn't know it was going to be so short. Hardly up 'til it's time to come down again.' Nancy laughed in that brittle way people laugh when they know what they've said isn't particularly funny.

Eve looked around, wondering if there was anyone she knew

in the airport as she tried to make her encounter with Irma and Nancy appear as casual as possible.

Irma had none of the vulnerability people in transit often have. She was completely unselfconscious, dragging her suitcases behind her, seemingly unaware of the squeaky noise their back wheels were making. When she suddenly dropped the two handles at the exit doors and began offering insights into Eve's 'family pathology', Eve was hard-pushed not to apologise to the people who had to squeeze by. And Irma remained right there, describing Eugene Wall and Mary Byrne as Doyle rejects, prototypical victims of the nuclear family's impulse to protect itself against interlopers. The impulse, she said, was most pronounced in patriarchal societies where material wealth and individual status were synonymous. What Eugene and Mary had in common was rejection. Eve tried to concentrate as Irma leapt from one syndrome to the next – mutual pain, subliminal quest for revenge, negative attraction. Standing at the exit doors in the airport, Irma's insights sounded altogether different to how they had sounded back in Raleigh Reilly.

As she drove down Patrick Street, Eve looked out at the people, vaguely following the path of a woman laden down with supermarket bags, unable to share in the excitement with which Irma was charging her analysis. Eve began to point out the sights, rolling down the window to see if the city's church bells could be heard chiming. She feigned frustration at not being able to change lanes, said off-hand, irrelevant things about her mother which she instantly regretted. But nothing that she or Irma or Nancy said could save their conversation from trickling to a standstill. It was as if they had all failed to live up to expectations. Then to Eve's surprise, Irma turned to her in the hotel lobby and, looking much older, almost aged, said to her in a defeated drawl.

'Look dear, we're tired. There's been a lot of travelling and the Veil conference, it … I think the best thing for us to do right now is rest. You tell me what time you're going to call by tomorrow and I'll be ready,' and with a smile and a lot of effort she added, 'fresh as a daisy.'

Eve hadn't even mentioned that her mother and Aunt Mona had supper waiting for them at Mona's. She stood watching as they were led away by a porter whose flirtatious 'this way ladies – if you please' left both of them visibly nonplussed. Eve waved as they followed him into the lift, both by now keen to tell each other that Eve had lost a lot of ground since she got back.

Eve had not expected to be plagued by new doubts once Nancy and Irma arrived. It took her the full length of the journey back to Mona's, twenty minutes, to persuade herself that involving them was a good idea. What saved her from believing that she had made a mistake was the memory, still an immediate source of anger, of Mary Byrne's reception at The Acre on New Year's Day. Eve felt implicated in the cruelty with which she had been treated and often relived the afternoon, casting herself in a much more assertive role. If nothing else Irma was bringing Mary Byrne together with the Doyles and that alone, Eve told herself firmly, justified taking up the offer of help.

Mrs Doyle and Mona had spent all morning in the hairdressers and all afternoon preparing an elaborate fork supper, now laid out on the mahogany table behind the closed doors of the dining-room. The room had not been used since the previous Christmas and normally would not be used until the following Christmas. Mona, who had been persuaded by Mrs Doyle to change into slacks, was uncharacteristically excited. There was something daring about using the dining-room in the middle of the year and she kept peeping in to have a look. Once or twice she ventured in and approached the crockery and dishes with that mix of wonder and fear with which small children approach things they are not supposed to touch. She took particular pleasure in running her finger around the rim of the big black ashtray which had not been out of the sideboard since Frank died. It was his favourite, deep enough to leave his pipe on without it toppling to one side. She was on one of those secret visits when she heard Eve coming in. She stood rigid as though she had been caught red-handed stealing the plate of butter pats she was admiring.

If they were disappointed when Eve told them that Irma and Nancy were too tired to come to supper then it was not apparent. Mona immediately reverted to form, clamping like a shellfish, relieved to drop the mask of good humour. Mrs Doyle took it as a challenge, an opportunity to display her skill at salvaging a whole meal and keeping it on hold until it was required. Twenty-four, thirty-six, even forty-eight hours later she would be able to re-create it, fresh and crisp as it was at that moment. She already had a plan but it couldn't be disclosed because it threatened to break one of the many ground rules Eve had laid down about the conference. No food, not even tea. Eve had explained that any person providing an unremunerated service, like tea, to a group automatically precludes themselves from being treated as an equal by the rest of the group. Mrs Doyle had agreed as she always agreed, but confided to Mona later that she had her pride and was not going to let a whole group of people, some of them strangers come and go at The Acre the following day without so much as a cup of tea. As was often the case, Mrs Doyle's cup of tea was a metaphor for much more lavish hospitality.

Eve had taken care to explain that the following day, July fourth, was an opportunity to clear the air, to get things on to a more realistic footing. Mrs Doyle accepted that but somehow had got it into her head that it was going to happen as a result of everyone just meeting, a small family gathering to entertain two of Eve's American friends, with Mary Byrne mingling inconspicuously among them.

It was to make the get-together a success that she set out for The Acre at six a.m. the following morning with the fork supper expertly packed in an assortment of tupperware boxes.

167

Once there she stoically set to work cleaning. She knew, from her short visits, just how bad things were. If she had allowed herself to think about it she might easily have been overwhelmed. So she just set to work, starting with the kitchen. She vowed herself to secrecy on the state of the sink and on the bin which had become an area rather than a container. By offering up her disgust, she was able to get through the worst of it. By seven forty-five she felt she had made real progress, at least with the surface areas and was almost in a position to start getting things ready for breakfast.

Unable to wait until later she had taken a step, a big step back into her life, one which by eight o'clock, when Mr Doyle sat eating the boiled egg she had cooked for him, had become an enormous leap.

He helped her to bring the tupperware boxes in from the car and under her supervision, put them down gently on the newly cleaned kitchen counter. The way he stood, supplicant like a question mark, mutely asking what he could do next, prompted her to tell him that Eve would need the car to collect their guests that afternoon, adding, when he went to look for the keys, that there was no point in bringing it over at that stage because she wouldn't be up. Anyway there was too much for him to do. All morning they worked together like a team of plough horses busily restoring The Acre to its former pristine condition.

It went so fast that there wasn't time to stick to the plan of dropping the car over to Eve, at least not in time for her to drive Mr Doyle back and then go on to collect Irma and Nancy as arranged. They had to drive over in tandem with Mr Doyle popping his head out the window of his car explaining to any motorist who tried to come between them that they were travelling in convoy.

On the way back, Mrs Doyle resisted the urge to tell him what he ought to wear that afternoon. Instead she announced that she was going to take Italian lessons that winter and in the late spring hoped they might go to Venice. His eyes shot to the side of their sockets and without moving his head he scrutinised her, looking at her in profile, every feature, as though he was seeing her for the first time. But it was not at all peculiar to Mrs Doyle as she sat there thinking about gondolas and humming an aria from *Il Trovatore* that she should have reached such a point with so little conscious thought or discussion. There were, she instinctively knew, certain journeys that were ill-served by maps, however accurate.

'We figured it out OK,' Irma said, as soon as she got into the car. 'Took a while, but we got there.' She turned around, not so much looking for agreement as giving Nancy an opportunity to agree, before she continued. 'I was experiencing bilateral conflict when you came to collect us at the airport yesterday. I guess you must have noticed how I was struggling to reconcile the persona on vacation with the inadequately briefed facilitator.' Irma began to laugh. 'If you think it was uncomfortable to witness then you can imagine what it was like being the actual site of such a battle. What's worrying is,' and she remained poised on the *is* while she began to root in her bag, 'that long after Nancy had produced the evidence, proving – unequivocally – that I was experiencing oh hell, you know where this is getting us? I'm falling into the same trap.'

'No you're not, it just feels like that,' Nancy said calmly. 'Falling into a trap – once you know it's there – is different. Some part of you has decided . . .'

'What a beautiful view of the ocean,' Irma sighed. 'Just look at that. Do you think we could stop? I know I'll regret it if I don't photograph it.' Eve pulled in straight away, telling Irma as she did that it was a sea, not an ocean, pleased to postpone their arrival even for a few minutes.

Mr Doyle, dressed in a dark navy suit and compulsively fingering his tie, stood on the look out at the front door of The Acre. When he saw the white Mini approach, he walked down the drive to welcome them, his arms high in the air. Eve wanted to warn him that charm, which he sometimes used in absurd quantities to win the confidence of women he regarded as difficult, might not succeed with Irma and Nancy.

'*Céad míle fáilte* – a hundred thousand welcomes as we say in Ireland.'

'It's OK. I can get out of the car without help.'

'Dick. Dick Doyle. Yvonne's father.'

'It may appear ungracious,' Irma was at pains to sound reasonable, 'but we're running to a format this afternoon. There's a built-in slot for introductions, a context designed to give everyone an equal opportunity to say who they are and what they hope to achieve by participating.'

Mr Doyle withdrew his outstretched hand. Nancy's vague smile did little to offset the disbelief with which he looked at Irma. He walked ahead up to the front door and stood back with exaggerated courtesy as Irma and Nancy walked in, determined not to take issue with every attempt he made to force them into gender strait-jackets.

'Which of them is the psychiatrist?' he whispered urgently to Eve as she passed him.

'Neither,' she said, glad she did not have time to elaborate.

'By the way, Noel rang,' he said as he closed the front door. 'He and that *amadán* he brought here at Christmas are on their way. They'll be late, he said to go ahead.'

Inside Mrs Doyle was standing in the hall, her eyes beaming like car headlights but with her mouth so tightly closed that even someone meeting her for the first time, as Irma and Nancy were, would sense that she was trying to keep something in. Her effort became the focus of everyone's attention when Eve asked her if there was something wrong.

'She brought Eugene with her. He's in there with her. Holding hands.'

As Mary had not said anything about bringing Eugene, it took Eve a moment or two to see it was as an acceptable step for Mary to have taken. If, as the familiar voice of reason asked, everyone else was accompanied, why should Mary be alone? The more she thought about it, the more she took issue with herself for not suggesting to Mary that she could bring someone if she wished. Eve might well have continued along that track if Mrs Doyle's distress had not become the event of the moment, touching Irma and Nancy very forcibly. Eve felt they were overreacting, carrying on as if her mother were in danger of collapsing. Nancy had her arm around Mrs Doyle's waist from one side and on the other, Irma stood leaning forward looking straight into Mrs Doyle's face with her arm squarely around Mrs Doyle's shoulder. Mr Doyle was looking on, frightened that there might be something very seriously wrong with Mrs Doyle, something which they saw but he didn't. They were whispering to her and among many other possibilities it crossed his mind that they might be saying an act of contrition into her ear, but he didn't have to consider that for more than a split second because it was immediately followed by the thought that they were highly unlikely to be Catholics.

Irma and Nancy, though sympathetic to Mrs Doyle's feelings about Eugene and Mary, suggested that she would be disadvantaged if she were to walk into the room supported by them. Both were thrown by the speed with which she took their advice, springing into an upright position, leaving their arms as though she had been mechanically ejected.

Eve took the lead by announcing to the small group, Mary, Eugene, Dr Wright, Mr and Mrs Doyle, Irma and Nancy, that there would be no introductions until a circle had been formed and everyone was sitting down. Mrs Doyle set about moving chairs as if she was organising a game of pass the parcel at a child's birthday party. She had found a way of joining in on her own terms. Regardless of how much at variance it was with the aims, procedures, ground rules and targets that were subsequently outlined by Irma, she managed by and large to adhere to it.

At one point during Irma's introduction of herself, Mrs Doyle did get a little uneasy. Irma had said that she hoped other members of the group wouldn't perceive her as a *deus ex machina*, capable of solving all the difficulties the Doyles were encountering. Mrs Doyle wanted to say that they were the happiest family in Ireland but challenging a person while they introduced themselves wasn't allowed.

Irma went on to say that she hoped she could provide a stepping stone to harmony based on genuine equality but didn't fully win Mrs Doyle's confidence until just before it was Mary's turn to introduce herself. Proceeding as sensitively as possible, Irma succeeded in getting it across to Mary and Eugene that they would have to sit on separate chairs. Mary had been sitting on Eugene's lap with both his arms around her waist, holding her like a very fat man might hold his tummy. Under normal circumstances, their sitting on top of each other like that would have been declared unacceptable by Irma at the outset, but because of Mary's vulnerability within the group Irma had decided to tolerate it until it was Mary's turn to speak. By that stage Mary, like most of the others was getting the hang of things and was happy enough to sit on the empty chair beside Eve. The one who was not at all happy about the arrangement was Eugene. Mrs Doyle had been willing the separation since they arrived at The Acre and when Irma succeeded in bringing it about Mrs Doyle felt she had done it entirely for her sake. Short of applause and cheering she did everything in her power to thank Irma.

'Thank you, Mary,' Irma said sweetly when Mary said her name and out of habit rattled off her address and her date of birth and when Irma remained expectant, her phone number.

'Now maybe you'd like to tell the group what you hope to achieve by participating?'

Mary looked at Mr Doyle who began to smile awkwardly at her. In the same instant, he was distracted by Dr Wright, who, with his hand over his mouth, very quickly whispered something in his ear. Both men then assumed positions which implied that the exchange had never taken place.

'I'm here for the same reason I came the last time.'

'And would you like to tell the group what that was?'

'Just to ... I had bronchitis for months and the doctor, she ... we had talked about it before, I mean meeting.' She gestured to the group. 'It was a New Year's resolution.'

'Excuse me,' Dr Wright waited until he had the attention of the whole group. 'I'm a doctor and I would consider it...'

'Can you wait please. The group will be happy to share your experience when Mary has told us a little about herself.' Before she had finished speaking Irma turned her attention back to Mary. Dr Wright then whispered from behind his hand again, furtive as a schoolboy. Mr Doyle shook his head.

'How do you feel about being here right now?'

'Fine.' Mary smiled over at Eugene who smiled back.

Irma had explained that in the interest of equality titles such as Mr and Dr, badges of authority, would have to be dropped. When Mr Doyle, keen to be agreeable, chipped in 'That's fine by me, Dick's the name' Irma shook her head. 'Sounds as if I'm being negative here, but no diminutives. They suggest intimacy which can be alienating for others.' From that point onwards he was called Richard by Irma. On the same principle Dr Wright became Arthur.

She was on the point of giving him the go-ahead to contribute, to continue what he had been about to say about his being a doctor, when she detected that Mary might have something more to say.

'Are you sure you have finished telling the group what you hope to achieve by participating? And while I have the opportunity I'd like to say that I admire your courage, I think we all do, in coming along. It's a life choice you won't regret.'

Mary was hesitant but not uncomfortable. She looked first at Irma, then at Mr Doyle, trying to decide which of them she was going to address.

'I'm getting married. We're getting married.'

Eugene sat forward on his chair, ready to receive congratulations but slid back when he saw how fiercely Mr Doyle was scowling at him.

'I think the group is aware of that.' As she spoke Irma looked at each member of the group and encouraged them to nod with her. All, except Mrs Doyle, did.

'No. I know they know. That's not it.' Mary persisted. 'What I was going to ask...'

'Can you please stop talking.' Irma's voice was tightly controlled until she got to 'talking' when it soared up the scale almost becoming a roar. Mr Doyle and Dr Wright – Arthur and Richard – had been whispering. Both jolted with fright which seemed to kick-start Mr Doyle.

'If she or her mother thinks I'm paying for that wedding then they have another think coming.' Mr Doyle folded his arms. Defiant.

'Richard. Will you please apologise to the group.'

'He won't.' Arthur sprang to his feet. 'And he shouldn't have to. Paid her far too much in the first place, that's the problem. He could easily have denied it. And nobody would have been any the wiser.'

Mary had begun speaking before Arthur finished.

'I'm not asking for money.' She smiled in disbelief. 'I was going to ask if he would mind giving me away.'

Irma clasped her cheeks with her hands, unable to contain her shock. Eve decided to intervene.

'She means she would like him to lead her to the altar on her wedding day.'

'I think she knows what Mary means,' Nancy said, happy to speak on Irma's behalf until she regained her voice.

'Would you like to explore why you want him to give you away?'

Mary shrugged her shoulders, embarrassed that her request was coming under such scrutiny. Irma, thinking it was just a question of time before Mary understood the significance of asking Mr Doyle to give her away, began to nod encouragingly at her. Bewildered by Irma's coaxing, Mary shrugged her shoulders a second time.

'Give you away?' Irma said, emphasising every syllable and leaving long gaps between the words.

Before Mary said yes she looked around, wondering if the others were as perturbed as Irma seemed to be. When she saw that they weren't she said yes again.

Irma braced herself to speak but failed to say anything. In her confusion, she beckoned Eve over. The urgency with which she whispered muffled what she was saying and Eve had to lean down to hear her properly.

'I didn't realise that she was going to want . . . can you believe it? Such a flagrant need to repeat the experience of being given away? Doesn't anyone know it's a syndrome?'

'Maybe we . . . you should wind things up.'

'I couldn't do that, not at this point, it would be disastrous to leave so much unresolved.'

While Irma and Eve were speaking Mrs Doyle quietly crept into the kitchen.

'Before we get to the question of the wedding,' Irma stopped to draw breath, pleased to have said the word wedding without revealing her distaste for the idea, 'maybe it would be constructive to look at the circumstances of Mary's conception.' Irma seemed unsure of how she ought to proceed. 'You don't have to volunteer information,' she said warmly to Mr Doyle, 'but anything positive you have to say about it would contribute considerably to Mary's self esteem.' She smiled at Mary.

Somewhere in the audible breath Eve exhaled was the word fuck. She tried to conceal the mounting panic she felt at the prospect of hearing her father speak about Mary's conception. All her earlier reservations about letting Irma get involved returned, rushing headlong in a single torrent, sweeping away whatever benefits she had ever believed there were to the scheme. She wanted to call a halt, shout stop, but knew that if she did Irma would immediately launch an investigation into her motives. That moment, sitting there on the edge of her chair desperately trying to indicate to her father that he did not have to talk about – that he should not talk about – the circumstances of Mary's conception, broke out of the sequence in which it had occurred and went on to become the memory around which all other memories of that afternoon clustered. It never wholly lost its power to unsettle Eve, triggering, down through the years, the occasional bout of remorse; a feeling she invariably countered by conjuring up an image of herself as she was on that afternoon, earnest and hopeful, home from Raleigh Reilly. Not that there was much room for remorse, or any of its allies, in the life Eve went on to build for herself. Hers was a world where personal development was monitored as closely as someone of her mother's generation might have monitored a burgeoning romance. Remorse, guilt, regret were scotched on first sighting.

Events at the Acre that afternoon became a story Eve enjoyed telling because it marked a particular stage in her own development. In the same vein the long self absorbed, Christmas PC print-outs which Irma sent became annual reminders to Eve of how much more progress she had made compared to Irma. Among Eve's friends, particularly those with whom she discussed and plotted her life course, Irma became almost a figure of fun, someone they saw as hopelessly stuck at the starting tape while they surged ahead.

For her part, the world Irma had stumbled into on that day at The Acre seemed as much in need of radical overhauling as the most underdeveloped of the Veil countries. She wrote a paper on the experience which was published in the Veil journal under the title 'The Chameleon Revolution'. In it she drew particular attention to societies which take legislative steps to eradicate inequalities without making any attempt to tackle the cultural practices which keep them in place.

Mr Doyle responded to Irma's request to talk about Mary's conception by saying that he had no objection to giving her away on her wedding day. As he spoke he became more despondent, seemingly overwhelmed by something greater than the circumstances confronting him. There were ever widening gaps between his words, which soon petered out altogether, leaving him stranded on the word 'I' as though he had lost his voice. But while there was a marked air of defeat about him, defeat itself was nowhere on his horizon. It was somewhere very far away, an unknown land from which he was separated by a vast ocean of self pity.

Following a second request from Irma, he broached the background to Mary's conception, but faltered so much that Arthur intervened.

'He did it on medical advice.'

Irma put up her hand.

'Do you wish to continue, Richard?' she asked Mr Doyle, whose head was bowed so low that his face could not be seen. When he did not answer Irma asked Arthur if he wished to say something.

'He did it on medical advice.'

'Please tell the group what was done and on whose medical advice.'

'Angela had a hysterectomy after the birth of her last child.' Long used to the silence words like hysterectomy commanded Dr Wright composed himself in the way a person might if they considered they had had the last word. Lips shut tightly, arms folded, entrenched expression.

'The group is not making the connection,' Irma said patiently and then with more bluster than the group had come to expect, 'and I'm not either.'

'I said his wife had a hysterectomy after the birth of her last child.' He emphasised each word, giving the group the impression that stupidity was at the root of their failure to understand what he was implying.

'Can you please be more specific.'

'He was advised. Medical advice.'

'From you?'

'Any doctor would have given him the same advice.'

'What advice.'

'To do the decent thing.'

'Is this some sort of game. Just what are you talking about? What is the *decent thing* he was advised ... you advised him to do?'

'Not to insist on his conjugal rights for a while. To make other arrangements.'

All the colour drained from Eve's face as her anger gathered in a tight knot at the back of her neck. Looking at her father, his flushed head fissured with thin strands of hair, like a fallen Humpty Dumpty, she put both hands up, urgently indicating to Irma that she wanted to call a halt.

In the silence which followed, Mary stood up and, looking only at Eugene, walked over to him and backed down on to his lap. Then they began whispering, a prelude to a series of quick, pecky kisses.

Irma and Nancy turned to each other, registering the same level of helplessness about what was, they told each other with doleful eyes, a tragedy.

Dr Wright felt that he had won the day for Mr Doyle. His victory was, he considered, so complete that he felt he ought to downplay it. This he did by masking his self-satisfaction with doubt, fingering his chin while he pretended to give the subject further thought.

Behind the kitchen door Mrs Doyle was listening, not to what was being said, which she was not able to hear, but for the right moment, a lull in the talk, when she could bring in the tea.

As soon as the kitchen door opened, Dr Wright swung around.

'Ah, Angela. Tea. I can't think of anything better.'

She backed into the room with the tray, anxious to tell Irma and Nancy that she had coffee as well and equally anxious to avoid censure from Eve who had been so emphatic, unpleasant to Mrs Doyle's way of thinking, about not serving refreshments. Incredulous, Nancy and Irma watched her rest one side of the tray down on the sideboard, waiting as she had so often waited for someone to finish taking their turn in a game of Scrabble or Monopoly. Flexible as always, she feigned the sort of tolerance she considered appropriate in emancipated circles as she looked momentarily at Mary and Eugene. She had, more than once, arrived in with refreshments to find a teenage game like Spin the Bottle or A Love or a Dare at an advanced stage. And while she was fully aware that neither of these games was in progress, her tolerance and good humour sprang from confidence. She was an old hand at intervening in party games that were going too far.

'Ahem,' she said as she carried the tray from the sideboard to the low table. 'Time for coffee. Eugene, would you mind moving the fruit bowl so as I can leave this down. It's as heavy as lead.' Her business-like approach prompted everyone, except Mr Doyle, to make co-operative movements and sounds. Eugene emerged from beneath Mary and after a brief moment of reorientation, he was helping with the same yes-Mr-Doyle-no-Mrs Doyle enthusiasm he had always carried out the chores she gave him.

Noel and The Saint arrived. And soon it was, as Mrs Doyle often said herself, 'all go', business as usual at The Acre. The clattery way she poured tea and the bustle with which she passed milk jugs and sugar bowls created a busy din. And, underscored as it was by her own pleasant chit-chat, it took on that warm hum she associated with happy homes. Only one difficulty remained. How, without antagonising Eve, was she going to get the group to the fork supper she had laid out in the dining-room?

The full impact of that afternoon's events on Mr Doyle

were not immediately apparent. For days he battled with the experience, struggling to keep it from linking up with the many other episodes which, since his retirement, left him feeling dispossessed. There was no single moment of defeat. It set in gradually, leaving him slumped in the roomy upholstery of the big green chair, silent and glum. There, betrayed by the world, stripped of his stripes for no good reason, he nursed his disillusionment.

In a flotilla of hats, Mary Byrne and Eugene Wall were married in The Church of The Holy Name that autumn. Mr Doyle was ruled out of the picture by Bernadette Byrne. Eve spent days agonising about how she was going to convince Mary that she was turning down the invitation to be a bridesmaid as a matter of principle. It was not an office she felt she could, in conscience, accept. Mary, lost in a whirl of excitement in the weeks leading up to her wedding was not put out by anything, least of all by the long letter Eve wrote explaining her position. Eve did, as she said she would, attend the wedding. She was placed at the VIP table beside Mary's aunt who kept reassuring her that her turn would soon come. 'One wedding always leads to another,' she said, surveying the room for eligible men for Eve. Self restraint and the belief that she was on a superior course stopped Eve from voicing the defensive thoughts that crossed her mind.

If she had found herself in a similar situation a year or two later her response would have been a good deal less restrained. She would probably have laughed and might even have said that she preferred men who were ineligible; nameless men who at the first glimmer of daylight would leave her apartment and return to wherever they came from, town houses, mothers or wives in the suburbs.

Eve continued to consider Mary as a worthy cause, someone who as a matter of principle ought to be included in Doyle family gatherings. Mrs Doyle was outrightly opposed to the idea, but at Eve's insistence, invited Mary and Eugene to call for coffee a few weeks after they returned from their honeymoon.

They stood at the front door of The Acre, unnerving Eve with their gratitude. Once inside they started to go through their wedding album. Through a series of fidgety gestures, Mrs Doyle managed to convey to Eugene that he ought to introduce Mary to her. Thinking it a procedure expected of newly weds and anxious, as always, to please Mrs Doyle, he stood back and spoke formally.

'Mrs Doyle, I would like you to meet my wife, Mary Wall.'

Mrs Doyle shook hands with Mary as though she was meeting her for the first time.

Eve looked on, thinking the whole charade preposterous, but pleased with the way her mother, once formally introduced, was warm and welcoming. Eve considered it a personal triumph when at the end of their visit her mother invited them to lunch the following Sunday.

She felt she was making progress, teaching her mother to unburden herself of some of her hang ups. Not until Mrs Doyle began to invite them regularly did it become apparent to Eve that as Eugene's wife, Mary had acquired a status which allowed Mrs Doyle to disregard, totally, her original relation to the Doyle family. Confronted with such flagrant evidence of denial, Eve had to revise the optimistic opinion she had formed of her mother's progress.

Eugene's delight in the Sunday lunch arrangement was a source of similar delight to Mary. They were noticeably less casual about it than any of the Doyles, particularly Eve who came in a dutiful spirit and left wondering how anyone survives family life. The Walls dressed up, were helpful, agreeable and solicitous. Eve was pleased to see her parents so well treated but felt claustrophobic in the Walls' company and patronised by the indulgent way they listened to her views. They took her aside after the birth of their first child, a daughter, and explained that the reason why they were not going to ask her to be the godmother, even though it's what they both would have liked, was because they knew she 'didn't go in for that sort of thing'. What irritated Eve most was how unindividuated they were, the way they always answered on each other's behalf or tipped the general company off about what kind of mood the other was in. Still, despite the widening gap that stretched between her and them, she remained committed to Mary and, as a consequence, tolerant of Eugene.

Eve had put off the question of a baby until the employment profile report was complete. But because there was no break between its publication and the position she took up to put its recommendations into practice, the question was postponed again. Then she began to suspect that she might be subconsciously putting it off until it was too late so she began to chart her every thought on the subject. Soon those thoughts had taken over and were virtually demanding action, prompting her to consider the practicalities in detail.

The most difficult question, the one to which at first there appeared to be no satisfactory answer, was whether or not to disclose her plans to whoever she selected as the birth father. This question would have to be answered before she selected him because it would necessarily influence the choice she made. If there had been a man whom she could rely on to take a consistent interest in the child from a distance, then she probably would have opted for that. But there wasn't. The likely candidates, the responsible ones, were few and far between and on close inspection usually turned out to be emotionally weak. The one who came nearest to fitting the bill, Eoin Slattery, was a serious candidate for almost a year. In a veiled way she broached the question with him once or twice during that time and was pleased enough with his response. But as their lives became more entwined he got possessive, displaying a slightly paranoid streak which she found increasingly oppressive. She scaled down the involvement, reluctantly coming to the conclusion that she would be better off looking for another birth father.

The decision not to tell the prospective birth father, whoever he might be, of her plan to conceive, meant that there was an enormous field to choose from. That advantage offset whatever lingering reservations she still had about keeping her conception arrangements to herself.

One thing for sure about Mrs Doyle, she was very good with babies. Everyone said so. Eve knew it would take a while to bring her around but felt sure her mother would, in time, become a mainstay in the child's life, maybe even look after it on a regular basis. Eve had begun to consider her mother in that light, evaluating her suitability in the way a man of another generation considering marriage and a family might have done. That Mr Doyle had once been such a man could easily have crossed her mind but she was too carried away by her plan, far too excited by the idea of conceiving a baby, to think about that – or indeed any of the other ways in which her journey had come to resemble his.